the dying poem

the dying poem

ROB BUDDE

Coach House Books

first edition

Published with the assistance of the Canada Council for the
Arts and the Ontario Arts Council

NATIONAL LIBRARY OF CANADA

CATALOGUING IN PUBLICATION DATA

Budde, Robert, 1966-
    The dying poem / Rob Budde.

ISBN 1-55245-107-9

    I. Title.

PS7553.U446D94 2002   C713'.54   C2002-904112-0
PR9199.3.B764D94 2002

for D.

'Jump, man, jump, they say to him. And he, who is about to leap into the void, discovers that he must stand still so things will happen to him.'
— Luisa Valenzuela, *He Who Searches*

' ... death is extremist fiction, the world we do not know, a world we have not entered.'
— Aritha van Herk, *In Visible Ink*

Dee knows Henry has killed himself. 'Henry.' Out of nowhere, for no reason, she mouths his name and knows he has killed himself. The knowledge a sensation that rises – a new language, a barely whispered utterance. Then more, bursts of syllables, and these sounds form limbs, eyes, hunger. Dee's countenance, her stiff social exterior, so practiced and precise, remains undisturbed. It is 4:24 p.m. and she knows he is dead.

Henry. He is no more.

The knowledge, a shift in chemicals.

In that instant, the feeling fans up from her fingertips as if a cold glass of wine has just been handed to her. He is dead. The knowledge slides up her shoulder blades and settles around her neck. Henry is dead. She, outside herself, saying the words, 'He is dead.' This impossible knowledge coming to her without doubt. 'Dead.'

The word resounds. She remembers his face as he stands at her door that first night fifteen years ago. He is holding fruit, of all things: a pear, two peaches, a kiwi and a mango. They squirm in his hands like puppies and begin to tumble down the steps. His eyes are on his hands, trying to control them. His hair is unkempt and he is wearing the same clothes he wore the day before, cords and a baggy grey sweater. He seems ancient standing there, a stranded poet, decrepit and pure. Exuberant Athens, brooding Milan, weary London – any setting would have held him. He is a product of Western history standing there on a rainy night in suburban Toronto. He is a lyrical figure of speech, breathless and confident.

It is not raining but it should be. Standing on the steps outside her door, he knows she is watching his face and will not help him with the fruit. Even though she stands barring the door with her arms crossed, he knows she will let him in and tell him what mango trees look like. His eyes flash open as he tastes one as if for the first time. Then, he tells her how desperately he wants to be a great man, how he wants people to remember his name, to read his writing. She is stunned by his blunt honesty but does not believe him. Instead she humours him, shushes him. Makes love to him. This last she does reluctantly, knowing it is a trap, knowing that men like him build monuments around their lovemaking, as if it is something significant. He does not know how to make love very well, she thinks afterwards; he has a lot to learn about subtlety. She does not tell him this but instead looks across the bed with pity, wondering if she should try to save him. He is dozing off.

But this memory now teeters on the edge of absurdity. He is dead. That first night, even though in the past, sits precariously present on the edge of the idea of his death. That chasm, billowing into her imagination, swirls to fill all her concentration. And it is concentration. Part of her consciousness has followed him. She is curious more than anything else. Dee's mind addresses knowledge as if it were an intruder, as if she has caught language in her backyard late at night, as if it stands between her and peace. The loss of Henry seems almost trivial in the face of the question.

Yes, the question. She stops and looks directly into a lightbulb in the lamp beside her. She is not sure where she is for the moment. Her arm droops behind the chair and she lets her wineglass drop delicately onto the carpet. She does not even bother to imagine the red fanning out into the weave of the white berber.

The Goldheft Art Gallery reception is winding down, dwindling into cleanup. The cheese platters are nearly gone; glasses and smudged napkins cover the tables. The room smells like old wine on old lips.

While all this is swirling in her mind she has managed to shut out the gallery crowd. It does not take much effort. She has suspended a conversation with a Winnipeg editor who is probably going to ask her out for a drink. White salt stains spatter the bottoms of his pant legs. He published one of her short stories, a fairy tale that begins with a dream and ends in what then seemed like chaos. That was about three years ago and he has tried, in a cloying, pawing way, to keep in touch ever since. Henry has not come up in the conversation.

She leaves the party graciously. No one notices her change in mood as she pulls on her long coat and waves goodbye from the foyer. They mistake her urgency for an elegant exit and blame it on the demands of a literary star. They imagine the glamorous rendezvous she is hurrying off to.

But there may not even have been a change in mood. Dee puzzles over her reaction as she walks down the wet sidewalk to her sedan. If there was a change, it is from an absence, like from not eating enough. There is no shock. It is not surprising. It seems fitting.

As she drives, Toronto is reduced to light and dark shades, angles and space. She imagines what it is like to die as she descends under the Gardiner. Her thoughts straddle his image and the unanswered question of his absence. (There he is, smiling and bitching about something in the paper. His bathrobe is open and she can see his ribs jutting out of his lanky torso. His teeth are crooked, endearing.) How to be so lost in anything, so immortal, so caged.

As she re-emerges beneath the belligerent dark clouds, she begins frantically shrugging out of her coat. Like grappling with an attacker, she twists and lunges forward and to the side. The car swerves towards the curb. Finally, she tugs the coat free and shoves it out the window. It lands in the street like a body tumbling to a stop.

The streets are wet and empty and the dim outline of moon is jeering.

She vows to never speak of Henry again. Ever.

The Dying Poem:
A Film in Three Parts

Directed by Jay Post
Screenplay by Jay Post

I

Henry

DARK RED FADE-IN, as if vibrantly coloured shutters have opened into a brightly lit space, to a video camera and tripod standing against a sheet-draped background. A DRY, RATTLING HUM suggests the camera is running. Perhaps the camera is facing a mirror; perhaps a second camera is doing the filming.

A VOICE-OVER by a male NARRATOR begins.

> NARRATOR
>
> I should introduce myself. My name is Jay Post, the biographer, the documentary filmmaker, the exerciser of Henry Black's last wish. Or should I say exorciser – Henry

would love that. I am his killer, in a manner of speaking. This may be my confession. I have turned myself in. Book me.

Chuckle, then pause.

I am recording this after nearly having completed my work on Henry Black, his life and his writing – that will probably be on the cover of the film case: 'his life and his writing.'

I don't know what that means.

SOUND OF THROAT BEING CLEARED, as if disconcerted.

I want, as a closing gesture, to comment on life and writing. Black ended his life and ended his writing at the same time, one would think. But, here, near the 'end' of making my film, I begin to wonder about that word. I am thinking now of placing this at the beginning of the film, so it is both an ending and a beginning. We'll see.

I have been thinking a lot about haunting: how ideas, unfounded yet present, linger just out of reach; how people haunt in their absence by being achingly present; how time is haunted continually, cluttered up with ghosts and untimely appearances. We are haunted by things beyond us that may be just coming into view. My figchen, coming back after all this is over.

Pause.

> I wanted to capture haunting in this film. I have found that this is impossible. Ghosts, by definition, cannot be captured. So, I've failed. Thankfully. I think Henry knew I would; he imagined this just as I imagine him. The bastard.

It is clear, at this point, that the NARRATOR is reading from a script.

> Here I am, after talking through and prodding into and poring over and imagining and fingering and reconstructing and abhorring Henry Black's life, daring to speak of him as ...

Pause.

> Here I am reading him. And you, dear viewer, are reading me. I am imagining you in black clothing, in an aspect of mourning as you read me, as you watch this. Ghosts haunting ghosts haunting ghosts in turn.
>
> We slide through each other like vibrations, even while the world is ending.
>
> He is dead. He is no more.

FADE-OUT TO DARK RED. VOICE-OVER CONTINUES.

> I speak of him. I contemplate death, a tremu-
> lous voice, a fleeting, shrouded image in the
> distance, a faint sound, shuddering, just out
> of hearing …

TO BLACK.

♦

I don't think for a moment that I'm not going to fail at this.

The video footage is paused, his face frozen on the screen, eyes lazy, mouth open, one hand reaching in the direction of the camera, a gesture for emphasis. He is saying something passionate, but frozen on the screen it becomes a plea, a beckoning. The screen is stilled but flickering back and forth between two images a few fractions of a second apart, Henry's left hand moving a few inches and then back again in quick successive movements. His eyes are also flickering shut, open, shut, open. He wears a tired, tender expression that doesn't fit into the tenor of the interview waiting around this frozen portrait. A band of static snow drifts across the middle of the screen.

Looking at this image of the recently dead is disconcerting. I look closer, looking for the story to exculpate his death.

The photographs are scattered on my teetering coffee table, along with pages and pages of notes: biographical, from reviews and newspaper articles, scattered passages from his poetry. The place is covered with traces of him, layered with his face, his words, a shroud over my previous existence. I am staying up too late, to that point when ideas start swirling in beautiful but useless patterns. I want to turn Henry's life into a work of art. Maybe my life as well.

I suppose I want Henry to tell me what to do.

You see, this is a project of reanimation, of resurrection. Grave robbery. Placed in the amniotic light of film, the fantasized spark of life, Henry might groan to life. The clips and quotes stitched with narration form a new integrity so that he can stagger into my room and forgive my sins. My elusive companion, in theory, will no doubt make demands I cannot fulfill. I labour on, anyway. A kind of artistic suicide by accretion.

A documentary film profiling him will fail, I know. It will fail because the medium, the thin band of plastic, the light and dark frames, the soundtrack cannot contain what I desire. And even further, it will fail because what I desire is questionable, flawed from the start. Original sin in an agenda, an aesthetic preconception, an already skewed retina, an already tainted negative. I want to do too much – I know if I just stick to the formula, to the prescribed format of a biographical documentary, everything will be just fine. But I want to do too much. I know this, yet …

My living room is the only place I can work with the video and the printed stuff spread out enough to see all the parts at once. Even though the film was to be a straightforward documentary, I find myself sitting in my living room waiting for direction. Lying perfectly still on the hardwood floor, my body surging and undulating and gurgling, I reach out, listening, wanting to hear … what? his name? my name? the sound of thunderous applause? a confirmation? Yes, a confirmation is what I am waiting for. My body fills the room with impatient living. Supine, piteous, I wait. Read me a poem, Henry.

I am smoking too much, nicotine twisting my body like twine.

I can't let him become a puzzle.

I have arranged his books around me in concentric circles.

His doubly double face stares back at me from the screen.

Henry Black was a professor and poet, a romantic figure who captured imaginations but little attention. A 'romantic figure'? He would shudder at such prattle but it was part of what made him attractive and repulsive at the same time. He was famous for being rude and unruly, for keeping a bottle of scotch in his desk drawer, for trying to seduce his students. Writers imitated him and despised him at the same time. Fame eluded him but he lived it anyway. Fame eluded him but he sought nothing of the kind. He battled more elusive enemies than adoration or immortality.

While researching, I couldn't help but feel that I wasn't studying just the life of a man but the profile of an entire generation of artistic men. Or I was trying to make the story too big – it is a weakness of mine. Henry could easily stand for an entire grand tradition and his death for the end of that era. I was young enough to be his son.

I found myself looking at pictures of him, comparing the way he dressed to my own clothes. It irked me that his aesthetic sensibilities attracted me. I should be more contemporary. At the same time, I wondered at my profound disavowal of him. I found myself thinking of Dr Jekyll and Mr Hyde, or Janus. How much of Henry was also part of me? An artist and a man – the whole history of men flourishing in the grand auspices of artistic fervour flows around both Henry and I. Henry and I standing on the same stolen ground.

I pounded my head like I was in school again; I argued with myself over how much I had learned beyond Henry. But then I remembered a poem called 'King Shit.' I pulled it out of the stacks.

> *corridors to walk or hide*
> *shifting beneath my neanderthal*
> *gait my substantial weight*
> *of deeds and letters — master*
> *of letters they call me*
> *out, mantled*
> *erupting*
>
> *a foray into the gaseous*

A glimmer suggesting we were made of the same stuff.

I found myself panicking a little. I could see my project dying a painful death, another film disaster looming. You see, dear patron, I had never successfully finished a film. I've started grand ventures filled with artistic frenzy and independent quirkiness. But, always, inevitably, I went too far, ran out of money, alienated the actors, the crew. Once I was left at a remote shoot, notes and scripts floating in the breeze, with the angry crew in vehicles disappearing around a bend in the gravel road leading (after half an hour of potholes and swearing over spilt coffee) to a small town consisting of a post office and a bulk gas station.

Scattered in my living room, I have one thirty-five minute videotape of interview clips, thirty-nine pictures, some posed, some snapshots, an uncooperative lover's address in Nova Scotia, a dismally thin and sporadic diary, a clog of old e-mail messages, twelve books of poetry and a suicide note.

His suicide crowds out all my research, becomes a vague but persistent background noise in the voice-over. That point of self-annihilation is where I had to begin. Endings, beginnings – a shimmer of recognition. Confirmation.

Am I wrong to make it such a juncture or pivot? Death seems so tumultuous, so pat, but maybe it's less cataclysmic, less profound. Maybe it's more like a tide, a slow dawning, a shifting light. A gradual change in the quality of light. That is what I want to reproduce in narrative.

I always construct a flow chart for my films so I can see their shape, the movement of their parts, the accumulation of images moving towards that perfect question on the last sheet of computer paper. The one I have drawn up for Henry's documentary and taped on my wall drifts in and out of segments, dates, places, texts, and disappears into the last crude square that has only the date of Henry's suicide in it. This is where I have to begin – the day of his death. What happened that day, what was his state of mind, what precise intentions or desperate conclusions had he made, what were his last thoughts? Where was he going?

And where was Dee the exact moment he died? Was she here in Toronto? I move back along the wall to a page above my electric space heater. DEE is written in block letters over a list of her books, her birthday and a short list of dates: the day they met, trips with Henry, periods of time when they seemed to have split up, movements towards and away from each other.

But lives are not paths, they are immersions.

Smoke hangs in the room: ritual incense, the tomb of the occasion, the traces alive, soaked into the pores of my skin. I will have to start again.

Hours pass. I take down the pages on the wall and throw them in a green garbage bag.

Days pass. Light moves from sunlight to streetlight to sunlight. I drape myself across a chair but cannot face any writing. The room is a morgue. Finally, on the third day, I pick up a bibliography. It pulls me back into reality.

The stupor does not end easily. Almost as an afterthought, I turn the camera on its tripod so it points at the window, now the colour of one a.m. The bibliography is Dee's, her books and articles all neatly alphabetized. Standing near the window, I turn and talk, formally, stiffly:

'Dee received more publicity than Henry. Her books were more successful, picked up by bigger publishers, and her work was more often anthologized. I had read two of Dee's books before: a novel, *Lucid*, and a collection of short stories, *The Last Time*. None of Henry's books. Some of Dee's novels were even beginning to be taught in universities. *Lucid*, especially, was catching on in terms of reviews and awards and all those things that snowball into readers and fans. It was one of those books that competed completely and insistently with the flagrant chaos of the everyday. It was set in a lighthouse at the turn of the century and followed the movements and thoughts of two women as they watched a boat coming out from shore. Dee plays with all sorts of other texts, Woolf, Milton, de Beauvoir, but it is the intense concentration of feeling, especially rage, which flows from the fractured and charged activity of the two women that makes the text so memorable. The two women are named Sara and Lily and they do hardly anything but watch over the course of an early afternoon the approach of this small boat. A man and young boy move about outside the lighthouse and twice ascend, but most of the interaction is between the two women who are in love with each other and at odds with each other. Essays on the book describe it as a feminist *Waiting for Godot*. It's much more, though. It is brilliant.'

As I speak, I recall a short story called 'Tulia' in her book *The Last Time,* in which a small girl slowly works through the memory of her abuse and, in the storytelling, regains some sense of herself and trust in the world. I remember that story because at one point the girl (named Sherri, not Tulia – Tulia is the town she and her family lived in) attempts suicide with a razor blade to her wrist. It is a graphic scene that I won't soon forget. I wondered if that story entered into Henry's thinking about suicide.

'Dee was a hot literary commodity; her books always danced at the bottoms of the best-seller lists for a few weeks. She was always on reading tours and flying off to conferences in Europe and the States. Henry travelled, too, but more for strange research trips and escapes to inland Mexico and Portugal. He did the odd reading, frequented pubs, hung back at functions at which Dee was the star. He would hunch over beside the cash bar, grumpily bantering with some of the other older writers. He stared openly at the young women and would occasionally lean over and flirt with them. Henry was of that generation that became aware of the maleness they participated in and yet could not shirk most of its conventions.

'Henry and Dee fought openly in public – quick bursts of shouting, curses, and they would storm off in separate directions. Lovers or potential lovers would rush to console, scurrying off after them. At readings or openings, crowds would watch for the telltale signs that the angry fireworks were going to start. It became a spectator sport, and it was hard to tell if Dee and Henry knew this. They did not seem to notice the sidelong looks and the expectant hushes when they entered a room. The intensity of their gazes was saved for one another. Volatility seemed comfortable; it seemed part of the process, part of the performance.'

Pause. Sleep now seems possible. The camera left running, I slump into the chair near the window.

(Later, I find my shoulder still in the frame of the film and I hear myself talk in my sleep. Mumbling mostly, but this comes clear: ' … just sit still, ya bastard … stay still … the vein is up … almost … ')

♦

To the film company, Henry's life story was enigmatic and worthy of government funding.

The company's commission was specific in its insistence that the film be centred on Henry. Its application to the arts council for funding had been based on the project. I asked the Company Director, Desmond Carny, whether I should play his death as a symbolic resistance to government cutbacks in the arts.

He turned to me with a start. 'Heavens no, no need to make it political. It's a biography, Jay. Don't go off on your own. Just capture the man. No need to make it political.'

We stood in his office, which had no chairs, and frowned over each other's tendencies.

I knew that's what he was going to say. Desmond hired me five years ago; when he offered me the job I almost turned it down, knowing that it would be a struggle to work under the direction of the company. My creative freedom, whatever that is, was something I valued at the time and it was at stake. But I was also tired of being poor. I was living in a two-room attic apartment that I shared with several squirrels. The Italian lady who owned the house would come up when she knew I was out and snoop through my stuff, looking for drugs or something. The house sloped so steeply that a golf ball would roll and crash against the wall with a loud *thwack*. The house swayed in the wind, which was good for sleep but made me wonder about my safety. So, a compromise: the company set guidelines, and I would do what I could within those guidelines.

Capture the man. No need to be political. Those were the rules.

When I went to the office to accept the project, I found out that Henry had sent a letter to the company two months earlier proposing that they do a documentary about him. Even though I had never met Henry, the letter requested that I do the film. I looked up at my calendar – two months would have placed the letter the week of his death, maybe even the same day. Why request me?

Henry speaking to me from beyond the grave. A dying wish – a performance by me, for an ethereal audience of one.

♦

He did leave a note for Dee, written in overly careful printing, as if it would be a keepsake. It wasn't. If Dee went to his apartment at all, she did not take the note with her when she left.

I only found out there was a note after persistent phone calls to Henry's friends. Henry's sister finally gave me keys to his place and said Dee had given her permission to let me in.

His apartment was on Garden Avenue near the lake and a few blocks from High Park. He owned the top of a narrow terracotta-coloured house with riotous day lilies leaning over the driveway. Next to the back door, a trumpet flower sat just uncurled. On impulse I filmed a short segment of just the flower and, as I filmed, a cloud passed over the sun and the white turned a deep blue in the shade.

The kitchen at the top of the stairs was bare, hardly used. I had noticed his office and car seemed the same way, as if he didn't exist or somehow went through life without using anything, without leaving any imprint or wear. A calendar of Georgia O'Keeffe paintings hung by a large-faced clock. The calendar was open to March and there was a blue-white painting of a trumpet flower above it. I stopped again and filmed a brief segment of the print.

The living room was also nearly bare. A blue futon couch was stacked with boxes of papers that I had been given permission to take out with me. But it was the note I was looking for.

When I picked it up from a tiny end table near a shuttered bay window, it seemed warm to the touch, as if it had just come from an inner pocket. It was written on a plain white page carefully, meticulously folded in half and set so that one half raised itself slightly off the other. I picked it up as if it might dissolve:

> D,
>
> You are disappointed. You are frowning fero-ciously and cursing the day we met. I realize this and made the choice anyway. You will reconstruct my reasoning and see I have never been more foolish. This I know. But timing is everything: pace, breath, closure. I do not exist anymore and you are reading this and I am wondering what my relation to this text is. I am still lucid, writing this. You know that. I expect you will think about the same things. I am dead and you are reading my writing. 'Words are not love.' Maybe they are.
>
> I have always 'loved' you.
>
> 'Henry'

Besides leaving the note, Henry told at least a dozen people over the internet about his plans that day, although he didn't tip off anything unusual except maybe the ambivalent 'one more afternoon':

> off to sit in the northwest wing of my favourite build-ing. they're tearing it down the bastards. one more afternoon for reading. the sun will be slanting from that south window just in time to warm my spot.
> > > > socrates.

Some of the messages varied but most ran along the same lines.

Socrates was the name he used on the net. When I first went into his account I used his user ID and freaked out all his e-mail friends. They thought I was him come back from the dead. A poet north of Prince George in BC wrote frantic e-mails crowing about how he knew the news was a hoax and that 'he' (meaning Henry) was okay after all. Others wrote angry e-mails cursing the prankster who was sullying Henry's memory by impersonating him. Quickly, I switched to Socrates2 but everyone started referring to me as Plato instead so after a while I adopted that name.

The most apparent signs of Henry's presence in the apartment were at the computer. His computer smelled like old cigarette smoke. He smoked du Mauriers, his little red package around him all the time, on the coffee table in front of him, in his lap, tucked in his front shirt pocket. I thought of Anna Karenina's red purse when I saw it in pictures – Henry's little red purse. He smoked with flair, practiced at exhaling sculptures of swirling mystique. It dated him irretrievably.

There were brown stains on the A, S and delete keys. Brown-black, not like coffee but like old dried skin and sweat. The H key had to be hit a little harder than the others. The monitor and keyboard were perched on an old sewing machine table with a cast-iron foot pump, the mechanism swinging up from underneath.

I felt like an archaeologist sitting there, looking around the room as if sifting through layers of sediment. A fingerprint smudge. Empty bottles of Metaxa, sherry and dark ale. An elephant figurine covered with tiny squares of mirror and a red glass gem on its forehead. The statue of a black cat arching its back as only cats can. A gift from Dee? Hieroglyphs, runes. I felt like I was searching for the origins of mankind, not the story of one man.

Perched there, hands on the keyboard, I felt like I was Henry's ghost come back. Sounds from the street filtered in just like they would have when Henry sat here writing poems. I was tempted to turn on the computer and write a poem. I reached, stopped. I don't write poetry. That would be going too far. Too far altogether. I pulled my hesitating hand back.

♦

In 1982 and 1983, Henry spent nineteen months travelling around the world to research different ways of committing suicide. He travelled four continents, visiting hospitals and psychologists, cops and sociologists. The techniques and subtle variations intrigued him – he read the deaths as if they were ciphers. Plastic tubing. A forked incision. Alchemy. Genuflect.

In an asylum near Johannesburg he witnessed a double suicide. Two women jumped to their deaths after sneaking away from a cleanup crew on the grounds near the white-washed sanitarium. They knew they would never survive the dizzying drop to the rocks on the shore. They leapt together, not hand-in-hand but almost – as if they were thinking about holding each other but in the surge of the leap they lost touch. One could imagine they swooped away from the cliff and the rocks below, arced out into the open sea and plunged together into its green depths. Perhaps to become mermaids.

Henry spent three weeks lingering in the small town near the cliffs, as if he were looking for the ghosts of the two women.

He crouched in the café, the townspeople flowing around his watchful silence. The people were generally accepting of madness, knew it was part of the richness of life. The waiter brought him wine and coffee and later in the day a rice salad with sweet tomato and avocado. He was polite and let him stay, knowing it was good for business to have flamboyant visitors for the regular customers to watch. Henry studied the shadows of passing couples, the play of light off their buttons, the ruddy colour of the backs of their hands. He spoke to no one, fearing he would scare away the shy spirits he sought.

During the early evening, he hunched over town-hall records – the women's families, their arrests, who they voted for, how much property their fathers would not share with them. After dark, he wandered the streets like a ghost himself. The only tangible record of this period of time is Henry's sporadic and gnomic journal. I had his travel itinerary, but months pass with no other trace. Itinerary becomes meaningless in the face of the gaps.

In his journal, Henry dwells on them, records their names, Ndeleke and Sarah, describes them in detail, their dress, their posture as they approached the cliff edge. In later journal entries he copies out poems about lovers' leaps, the romantic vision of two lovers testifying to their devotion by being joined in death. He scribbles in the margins of the poems, crosses out words. He often notated texts this way, blotting out parts as if they were superfluous, as if by paring them away he could arrive at their essence. One of the poems was completely crossed out with only the name of the small town, Uddie, scribbled next to it.

Henry remained in pursuit of the idea of suicide. According to him, he never captured it. At least until his own.

While in Chicago in 1986, Henry bribed the police to call him to suicide scenes. He would arrive and hover around the apartment or alley, looking for clues, looking to the details of the act. He would overhear police interviews with family and neighbours and reconstruct the event on paper. After a few months these re-enactments gained sophistication enough that he began to write them in first person, from the point of view of the deceased: fictional suicide notes, final accounts of the gentle or shocking fall into nothingness. After a few months, he looked only for the unusual acts. He'd seen enough and now craved the exceptions, the oddly placed, the strangely dramatic, the unusually gruesome.

He witnessed all the radical display of the frailty of the human body, all the ways in which it can be undone, dismantled, eroded, corroded, oppressed, negated, slaughtered, expelled and expended. He retraced the steps of a jumper on Dearborn near Congress, carefully shuffled out onto the ledge facing the wall, crept to the jutting corner, leaned out to peer down twenty-seven floors to the cab-filled street below, felt the tug of the wind sidling by the building, scraped the caked pigeon shit from his shoes. He retreated reluctantly, dreaming of the precise parachute that could let him take that one further step .

In his journal was a detailed description of the colour and consistency of human brains. 'This,' he wrote, 'contains in code the wisdom of mankind, the gelatinous mess like a tiny decimated library scattered across linoleum.' He noted the way bullets often produce a tiny entry wound but a massive exit. What was their last thought? Is that the right question to ask? He pondered the reinvention of a dead psyche, retraced steps like he was editing a flawed narrative. Searching for that perfect last line.

He learned what chemicals can do to the body when ingested in large quantities. How the heart seizes, seizes, stops. How watching one's own body collapse can be hypnotic – each sensation greeted with wonder and curiosity. How the nervous system can be sabotaged, set off-kilter like a derailed train, how it careens off into immobility, the inability to hold onto the solidity of a heartbeat, breath, and we fly off into chaos. He pondered how methods (Henry vacillated wildly between scientific objectivity and lyric reflection – 'method' was a word he employed when he clung to the former) like overdosing, gassing in the garage, cutting wrists, drowning were most often meant to fail, a vital and desperate statement to the world meant for effect, meant to alter the person's future, not end it. He called these the 'contemplative methods.' He read how drowning was, perhaps, the most peaceful choice, one in which the last seconds are filled with coloured spirals and kaleido-scope patterns – a wet, exuberant return to the womb, Henry suggested, though he had both 'too Freudian' and 'cliché' writ-ten in the margins. Later he disputed this, realizing that the numbers of suicides by the supposedly 'more peaceful' meth-ods were staggering in their success. He studied how hanging can either break the neck or asphyxiate depending on the height of the drop and the nature of the noose. How a gunshot into the mouth or through the temple, or a leap from a build-ing or cliff were usually acted out in an extremely agitated state, the subject in the climax of trauma versus a thoughtful motion towards self-annihilation. The 'violent' methods were nearly all committed ('committed? like a crime?' he wrote) by men.

All these contemplations on self-annihilation he collected, ordered, catalogued, hoarded, pored over.

Even in my retracing of his research, I felt a strange vertigo, a blend of fascination and repulsion that drew me into the suicidal elixir. I sipped. Henry tugged at my shirtsleeve.

He chose none of these methods, though, instead inventing his own. As if to add a page.

The strange thing was that he made his death look as if it were an accident. Have there been more suicides like that – ones never thought of as suicides? A quick swerve into oncoming traffic. A fake stall on the tracks. A boating accident. According to Henry's research, the whole point of suicide was to let people know you had committed suicide. Suicide notes, the telltale signs – it was supposed to be clear. It was supposed to be theatrical, a message. You don't hide your own suicide; it denies an audience.

Instead, he made his death a poem.

That is how I knew it was a suicide even before I found the note. Poems don't happen just like that. Life isn't poetic unless it's in a poem first. Poems are created, man-made. They are premeditated, planned carefully down to the last detail, crafted in order to be read. When he died, he had three books with him, as if to fill an afternoon of reading, but I know he had already read them. They were for show. Three books he brought into the deserted Metropolitan Library.

It must have been for show.

I can see him now.

He is sitting cross-legged on the bare hardwood floor, his hands resting palm up on his thighs.

Do we all believe we are prophets?

The northwest wing of the Met used to hold literature and philosophy but now is empty. Emptier than empty, because the ghosts of books and voices can't even find purchase on the floor stripped of its red carpet. Not even the imprint of bookcases and traffic wear remain.

The arched roof is of wood and careful stucco painted a soft cream colour. Motes of dust drift across the strong shaft of sunlight that is pressing on the patch of floor where he sits. The sunlit portion of the floor is as long as he is tall and as wide as his shoulders. One book sits open in his lap, two others open on either side of him. He is looking into space, at nothing. In his mind is the composition of his death, the whole artful arrangement of his own demise. Everything I seek.

The room is a painting by Caravaggio; a splash of light, a crescendo of stained glass, and the rest is meaningful shadow, shade off shade, descending into deep black, the mass of humanity. Henry's face is apocryphal – saintly and orgasmic, yet struck with pathos. There is no turning back; this is the way it must be. Strike me down. His poem 'To the One' begins

> buggered by the passing minutes, I am
> just beginning to rise, full-throated
> a singing lamp quietly nocturnal,
> flickering the surface of solitude,
> flickering the face of mortality,
> sliding away towards more sightly things.
>
> I want to dwell only on the singularity
> of this thought.

On the library floor, his legs cramping up, he is missing his cigarettes. He did not bring them. Neither a wallet nor his cigarettes were found on his mangled body. The crisp air hurts his lungs.

He breathes slowly, evenly, and hears a low rumbling like the end of the world. Space, his existence, suddenly turns to stone.

Such is the sacrifice for poetry.

They recovered his ruined body almost twenty-four hours later. It was twisted and torn and only barely held together in places. When they uncovered him, his left arm was miraculously raised above his head into the tonnes of rubble. Stretched straight up, his hand seemed to be reaching to touch something. Or as if to catch something lost in that chaotic last moment.

A book was lodged in his chest.

My apartment is a morgue, my film a cadaver upon a table. What next?

♦

I returned to his apartment, his last abode, on Garden Avenue near the park. His house, the walls that held him in when he was tempted to disperse, fly to the winds; the tidy little habits that held him together. Until they didn't.

His place seemed like a strange signature, a code waiting for its creator to come and set it to use. A demure, habituated waiting. Houseplants lay dry and ashen. Flies congregated on the windowsills.

The trumpet flower had come and gone, a memory of whiteness.

Most of his belongings had been packed up: his books, dishes, clothes, papers – those things that are easily packed away, built to move from house to house, life to life. I admired his austere trappings; the bare rustic accoutrements of his life took little space, left little work for whoever was seeing to his things.

A pair of shoes, old loafers with thin unravelling laces, still rested near the door. An umbrella and tan trench coat hung, expectant, above them. The place seemed animate, hunched, saving energy until it could shift into motion around a hand, a shuffling gait. A rusted and bent spatula perched on the back of the stove. An old radio sat at the back of the kitchen table near the window. All the windows seemed sealed shut by layers and layers of paint around the sills, as if in preparation for entombment. And yet I felt very much at home. My shoulders loosened from their knots of tension and I felt like I could breathe more easily.

If our lives are a shrinking periphery, is my innocence an expanse to bask in?

I went up to his bedroom; I hadn't gone upstairs last time. It was tucked at the end of the hall next to a bathroom with old-style rounded fixtures and a tiny bathtub with curled legs and a corroded brass tap. Soap scum and old skin still caked the cracks in the tilework, around the sink drain. The body always, always leaves its mark. The window in the bathroom looked out over alley and I had a vision of Henry standing up naked in the tub and looking out at passersby. Odd.

His bedroom was painted in an unusual pink-purple with a flower-design border. One still-healthy dieffenbachia stood in the corner, big as a hat rack. On his dresser was a glass container filled to overflowing with change, paper clips, rubber bands, coupons and ticket stubs – all the things that he would tuck in his pockets during the day. I ran my hands through this detritus. One of the coins was blackened from fire so the polar bear and queen were hardly distinguishable. I picked it up and held it between my finger and thumb, but it was cold, without any residue of heat.

I looked up, surprised to see myself in the mirror.

I lay down in his bed and stared at the ceiling, stared into what he would have seen, the patterns of paint strokes, the imperfections, the play of the light as the day turned.

♦

The dynamite expert said it took two tonnes of explosives to bring down the Met. Because of its stone superstructure and Roman arches it took many smaller caches of dynamite to fell it completely. Newer buildings tend to have a handful of key points that can be targeted by the demolition company's planner. The Met was more stubborn, wily in its old age. Even in the age of progress and budget 'sacrifices,' a few structures made a noise when they fell.

I think the company was worried about lawsuits or something because they were very nervous when I talked to them. Defensive-type evasive. The man who checked through the building just before the detonation was sweating when he claimed over and over that he went through that room, that 'the guy' must have been hiding behind a broken bookshelf, the only thing left in the room. 'He must have been hiding, the idiot. I looked, I looked. I did my job. I can't be responsible for some nut hiding in a condemned building. His own fault. Nut.' He shook his head, angry and scared, not particularly sad.

A bulldozer pushing through the rubble had snagged Henry's body, tumbled it into the surface air. A foreman saw it, called the police. They shut down operations for a few days while the police figured out who he was. They identified him quickly – he had ID on him – but took a long time trying to reconstruct what had happened.

The book startled them all – a large hardcover lodged cleanly in his chest. It seemed otherworldly. It seemed like witchcraft.

♦

He wrote in his journal as if High Park were a lover: *Oh, those lips, they taunt me, threaten me with language. I stood in that spot again. The gorge below me and moving to surround me.* There may have been a lover, there, under the elms, up on the hill in the middle of the roses, down by the water and the ducks. *Love couldn't be so simple as to compass me, pass me like a path, soak through my clothes like sun or sweat. I remember most your tired eyes and the span of your wrist, smoke swirling around both.* He walked the park every week, making notes or musing and scribbling once he got back to his desk. The park spilled on to the pages, bright light green in spring, dark and lush in the weight of August, frail and tremulous in fall. It was hard to discern whether he was in love with the park or someone in it. *You are there waiting and not waiting at the same time, cold water that spills across my hand but cannot stay, I cup it there to my lips, but you are gone. Drunk on trace, I will wait.* The park seemed a sanctuary for him and, at difficult or stressful times, he retreated there to be by himself or to be consoled by someone. Up by the rose garden he stood, a lone figure waiting, the cool fall wind billowing his overcoat, buffeting his pant legs. Traces of rain. He waits.

The roses spoke. High Park sequestered his secrets in the sidelong looks of geese, the furtive steps of a lover in a long coat, the ringing peals of a church bell against the low clouds.

It should have been a place to meet a lover. Kiss. Share some bundled sandwiches and a thermos filled with gin. A place where breathing would change, waiting, waiting, and then the catch when the other strolls into view, apologizing for being late, but it doesn't matter. It should have been a place to linger and slide hands down the waist past the edge of inhibition. And then the kiss and breathing would again leap, oxygen dizzying, suddenly a near-toxic gas swooping into the lungs. Gasping, the manipulations of the clandestine, the frantic fingerhold of life. And it would not be unlike dying, there, as the figure strolls into view, places a hand on his hip, pulls gently on his tongue with cold lips. And then again, when the other strolls casually out of view, conscious of casualties but not looking back, not looking back.

In this land of poetry and lust there was only the mythical and the other. Nothing else plays.

I tracked hard and long looking for signs of passion, any evidence of a tryst. There were none. But his language, the poems of his time there, the park infusing his consciousness, all gestured towards a secret passion. I kept searching, haunting the park, my footsteps a strange echo. And, oddly, frequently, almost alarmingly, lovers or potential lovers approached me.

Often as strangers they emerged from a hedge and came close, began with a greeting inflected with promise, abandon, challenge. But sometimes, the approach was as if there were familiarity, 'Ha, yes, hello.' Then, usually, dismay – it was not as they thought. I was someone else. The rain abetted this twilight dance, blurring and distorting the occasional streetlight.

Only once was I certain I had encountered a lover of Henry. It was a luminous morning and the park was nearly empty except for the stray jogger bundled up with muffs. Near the roses there was a lone figure in a long coat sitting on a bench reading. When I approached, the figure looked up and I heard a sharp intake of breath. The beloved sat facing east, the broken sunlight making colours and textures difficult to distinguish. The face of the beloved (I will never forget the pure, unassuming, porcelain beauty of that face) turned towards me with the force of a ghost. The face of the beloved (pronouns fail, for I could not be sure whether it was a man or woman) opened into a quick succession of emotions: expectation, disbelief, suspicion and disappointment – all of these in full force passed to me over the few metres of walkway in less than three of my strides. I rarely initiated contact with people in the park but I voiced a soft 'Hello' as I passed. A choked reply, 'Yes, yes,' returned but with still no indication of gender.

Three things I retained in that instant I passed; three details stuck as I walked away. The beloved was reading a book of poetry, though I could not see the cover, folded as it was. It was a thin book, around seventy or eighty pages, and a glimpse of the left-hand page as I passed revealed an expanse of empty white with, I presume, print closer to the gutter of the book. The other detail that stuck was the burst of colours that crept up the wrists and neck; tattoos spilled from beneath the figure's heavy clothing. The last detail I caught as I was just about past the bench. Out of the corner of my eye I saw a blink of white which a few steps later recollected itself as a photograph held loosely in the figure's pale right hand, the hand not clutching the poetry. It wasn't until later in the walk that I filtered through the image enough to realize that it was a photograph of Henry.

Those taunts, they untool my language, lead me into a garden of eyes, moist coins. The bench is my life, my writing. We float over it, clutching the breath from each other's mouths. Roses fail. The geese turn into seasons. Your coat hides the sun opening iris opening thigh opening my feverish denial, here, irretrievably without you.

♦

Being in the hometown of a dead man is like trying to remember something you've clearly and definitively forgotten. The suggestion is there that something is eluding you, something is being sought after, but that evasive thing is, and will continue to remain, unattainable no matter what you do. No matter what.

I followed the trails through Toronto, Black's scent on everything. The bartender at the Queen's Head pointed to where he usually sat with his collection of sad dishevelled cronies. They were not as unruly as I would have guessed. As we drank together, they were quiet, sad, grumpy at worst.

Near the bathroom there's a picture of Black sitting at the bar on a tall stool. He looks genuinely happy. His pant legs are hiked up so that you can see his socks and his white hairy shins.

His legs are spread so there is an ugly lopsided bulge of crotch smack in the centre of the picture. His signature is over the crotch.

One of the illustrious drinkers was a young man, maybe twenty. He wore a fishing cap low over his eyes, those big cargo pants and sneakers. He didn't say much but when he did it came off as a strange combination of deference and anger, self-effacement and complete disdain. Midway through the evening he handed me a poem. This startled me and I wasn't sure whether to read it there or not. I did. It was a difficult poem and kept my reading off-balance. It had the words 'hover' and 'smoke' in it but it was more about love and writing. It sounded a bit like a Black poem, but more open, chaotic – things I found lacking in Black's writing, I realized.

The young poet watched me. He moved over so he was sitting next to me. He didn't make eye contact very often but said, 'You can call me JP,' and reached to shake my hand. His beefy palm was sweaty and I noticed there were many beads of sweat on his brow. It didn't seem hot in the bar to me. He appeared to be at odds with his environment and I suspected this was the case in any situation he faced. He exuded moisture like a sea creature, shiny, clean, waiting to be immersed again.

'I'm Jay.'

'Cool name. A poet? I know you're doing that documentary on Black but you write, too, right? You've got that spaced-out, faraway look groove thing going.' This was a good thing.

'Not really, although I suppose film can be close to poetry, no?'

'No.' He said this emphatically, angrily. 'Words, man.' He leaned close as if to pass me something precious to place under my tongue. 'Language is a drug above all – take it, take it. Let it enter your veins. Write yourself to sleep.'

He reached into his pocket and pulled out a bottle of booze and a small book. 'This is for you – a small mag some students and I put together last month. Black has a piece in it you might want to see.'

I looked at the cover; it had a young man sitting, holding a lollipop, looking profound. The magazine was called *Seizure* and had a green corduroy cover.

The older men at the other end of the table were bitching about big bookstores, throwing around Marxist maxims with aplomb.

'Hey, let's go out … ' and JP pinched his forefinger and thumb over his lips.

I had smoked a lot when I was in school but was out of practice so the weed soaked into me quickly. The Ontario sky raged purple and blue. I could hear Bloor a few blocks away. I had so much work to do but JP transfixed me with his bleary eloquence and his passion for writing. He was looking for something in poetry – some release, some divine ecstasy, some relief from the real.

'Now, let's go play some pinball and make some magic happen.' I followed JP into a basement with orange light. Silver balls spun on his fingers. As he played he said he wanted to be the grandmother of all poetry, he wanted to give birth to hosts of little poets and to suckle them on long fat bongs made from the failed pompous scratchings of old male poets. He grinned a wide grin at the machine as he said this, tickled with its impunity.

I asked him to write my obituary when I died, made him solemnly promise he would do it.

◆

December 1979 interview with Carole Jerle, Henry ends the session with this: *Writing is nothing but a way to evade the law ... you know, not the cops, but all the laws we follow ... it's escape, don't you see, a way out, entering that free space, creating rules but ones unlike normal laws ... I suppose desire, violence, illogic, um, the incomprehensible, for example, waste, waste, waste, all the things we can't abide, I write. I suppose we work out all the things laws suppress, I suppose. [chuckle] It's a fucking revolution, hmm.*

Judging from his voice, he seems drunk. It is one of the few times he does not seem evasive or defensive. Words slightly slurred, odd runs of intonation in his sentences. In all the taped images I have of him he seems disarmed, relaxed to the point of arrogance or nonchalance. Interviewers seem put off by this, as if they resent not intimidating him, as if they are not happy without control of the interview. He rambles, ignores questions, scoffs and snorts. I read this as a type of defensiveness – he is taking control of the interview so it will not go where he wishes to avoid. His nonchalance is a cover for profound anxiety.

But he does not speak arrogantly. In fact, he frustrates just as much by his waffling, his uncertainty. As often as not, he makes a statement and, just as methodically, takes it back. One might think he is toying with the interviewer, but I don't think so. He seems to be genuinely undecided about almost any issue. And neither does he come off as the tortured thinker beset with contradictions. He was more serene than that. In the interviews, he always seems to slouch to one side, leaning one way in a chair or ducking slightly, resting his weight on one foot or the other.

Cameramen have difficulty framing him properly.

II

Dee

I planned to drive out from Halifax in a rented Taurus with a portable video camera that I could operate on my own. By not bringing out a cameraman, I thought I would save a few bucks that could be put towards post-editing effects — you know, actual credits, maybe some tastefully arranged passages from his poetry scrolling down the screen. When I picked it up at the airport, the car smelled brand new and I fiddled with the console. I had never rented a car before. The company accountant assured me it was a reasonable expense when I called him in a panic, feeling guilty even before I had left for the airport. I still felt guilty, like I was getting away with something. This is my prairie-boy heritage. I fiddled with the motorized seat-adjust one more time.

I stopped in Halifax for part of the morning to pick up some supplies, and while I had breakfast on the docks, I studied the ferries lumbering back and forth from Dartmouth. Seagulls bobbed in the choppy water, which looked deep green despite what I'd heard about the pollution in the harbour. I scribbled a few notes on the sunlit table under the heading 'The connection between minds.' The salt air snapped and the ocean-spangled sun crackled as I took notes about the similarities between Henry and me. Aloof, hungry, cynical, romantic (I scribbled out that one, but then rewrote it), creative (small question mark after that one: what does that mean?), obscure (with a little arrow pointing up to 'aloof'), trapped, doomed, contrary (another question mark and the word 'always?'), tempted, poetic (his work or his life?), uncontextualized. After that I started writing phrases I associated with Henry but only got a couple, and then, surprisingly, I started to write a poem. I don't write poetry.

fearing silence, still water
a request for your presence rings,
the repetition faultless

once upon a time I
wanted to be in a fairy tale,
one about courage and marriage,
the two complicit by the end

now I sit frozen in terror
waiting for the toll that signals
my entrance into that fabulous evasion.

I considered leaving the poem on the table tucked under the plate but at the last moment plucked it up and shoved it into the maw of my pocket, hoping I won't have to consider it again.

I missed the highway off-ramp and ended up heading north towards Truro. It took me way too long to realize this and I muttered the entire half-hour it took to retrace my path. These subtleties the material world throws at me are maddening and it was only when I began thinking about the sound of the name 'Truro' that my nerves calmed.

Dee moved deep into the Annapolis Valley to an orchard and market garden. She planned to buy hay to feed the sheep in the winter and wanted to grow apples, broccoli, raspberries and pot. She tied up her hair with a ragged strip of burlap. The sheep were never trimmed and wandered willy-nilly onto other people's land. When I asked directions from a couple cutting wood in the ditch they scowled and told me how several of her herd had died on the gravel road that leads out from Waterville.

The place was perched high on the south hills (or 'mountains,' as they called them at the grocery store in Berwick) and looked over the valley. Neat orchards and dairy farms lined the road and dogs came loping out to chase me several times. I grew up on a dairy farm, so I felt rather nostalgic as I drove past the pastures and oak thickets. I prided myself on knowing that the dairy cattle I saw are called Holsteins and remembered fondly the smell of their cud as they chewed serenely in the milking stalls.

The gravel road was stuttered with washboard, and a passing pickup sent a stone that chipped my windshield near the wipers. Shit, now I'd done it. I'd broken the car. I'd broken my rented car. I fretted over how I would deal with the chipped windshield, the star-shaped break blossoming into a huge tangle in my imagination. Shit.

Then I found the place. I had to park on the road and walk in down a muddy driveway filled with deep ruts. The house was old and large, two storeys, and was white, although much of the paint was flaking away.

I could tell she knew what I was there for. As I walked up the path between the maples, I could see her face in the screen door. I wondered what she had heard about my documentary. It took me a few seconds to notice all the differences between her and the woman I had seen in the pictures. There was a smudge of dirt near her mouth when she held open the door. She was bigger, taller than I'd thought. In the pictures, ones taken before Henry's death, she looked haunted. Now, she did not.

Out of the corner of my eye I noticed a dead grosbeak by the steps. It had probably hit a window.

I told her my name, although reversed: 'Hi, I'm Post, Jay.' She nodded, unfazed, and shook my hand (although remembering back, our hands hardly touched, one of those handshakes that is more about the reaching out than the grip – there was no pressure at all) but did not say anything. After an odd pause at the door while we stood uncomfortably close, she asked me to come in and leave my shoes on. I became aware of how shiny my shoes were and wanted to quickly scuff them up. Jackets and overalls cluttered the entryway and threatened to tumble down off the hooks as I brushed past them. A dried vine with small pumpkins still attached hung next to the door. The house smelled like dirt, fruit and woodsmoke.

We entered the kitchen, where three cats lay next to a wood cooking stove. One of them was a huge tabby with no tail that gave me a funny high-pitched meow as I came near. He seemed to be smiling a big foolish grin.

'Thanks for coming,' Dee said, facing away from me. She didn't seem to mean it. 'Do you want some coffee or … ?' She tried to think of what else she had and couldn't, so left off her sentence at that.

'Yeah, sure, thanks for having me, I know it must be weird and all, but I think you'll like what I'm doing, and I hope you might have some input or something, Henry's important to me now … the name's Jay.' I forgot whether I had told her that. I stopped suddenly, feeling both like I was intruding and like she was intruding on my project.

She turned and looked at my hands which rested on the back of the chair I was planning on sitting in soon. Just my hands, and then she looked away again. 'I am sure it will be wonderful. I am not sure what I can do for you.' Her power was a quiet, sure one, not apologetic, but not self-aggrandizing either.

'You don't have to do anything, really. I just think a film on him needs to know a little bit about you.'

'So, the film is going to "get to know me," is it?' She made quotation marks with her two index fingers and grinned, I thought, though she was still facing the coffee pot. 'I am not sure I am comfortable being made a character in a story that is supposed to be about … about him. How do I know to trust you to be my maker?' She finally looked directly at me. 'Besides, I have vowed never to speak of him again.' She said this as if she just remembered it. Her gaze was unnerving and I realized I had been taking advantage of her averted gaze to look longer at her.

A spider plant hung over the sink and there was a list of things to buy stuck by a corncob-shaped magnet to the fridge. Three beets, still caked in dirt, sat on the counter. She came with the coffee and sat down, so I followed suit. The cat, the big one, got up, lumbered over next to my chair, and rumbled aggressively into my lap. He was a good twenty-five pounds and hung off both sides of my lap. When I began to pet him, his substantial claws dug deep into my thigh. I had little choice but to let him. From then on I always associated talking to Dee with a warm, delicate but insistent pain in my thighs. I never told her this.

When she showed me around the house I realized that I had come up to the backyard and she had met me at the back door. A driveway ran out from her front porch through the woods to another access road. Roads here seemed random and erratic to me, who was used to the neat order of city blocks and, before that, the precise regularity of prairie roads. So many turns and curves seemed unnatural.

There was no front yard as such, but a gnarled oak held up an old, elegant bench-swing that swayed slightly in the breeze. Much of the tree had been blasted away, probably by lightning, so that only a few large branches remained reaching out, making the tree seem off-balance.

The living room was long and had bay windows on either end; through one the sky was darkening into dusk and through the other it was midday bright. In a large murky aquarium in the middle of the room, goldfish turned to face us and followed as we walked by.

Much of the room was covered with herbs laid out to dry on newspaper. The scent was overpowering, dry and sharp.

Most of them looked black against the newsprint, like mad monstrous writing in thick, pasty ink. The floorboards creaked amazingly loud – no one could sneak through this house. I asked her what the hole in the ceiling was for and she told me it was to heat the upstairs because the furnace didn't vent up there; the heat was supposed to rise. She said it got pretty chilly.

She turned towards me. 'You didn't answer me when I asked if I can trust you.'

How do you answer a question like that? 'I don't know how to answer that. Are you going to tell me anything about him?'

'No. But you can still do the film, without me, without anything – you're already doing it without him, aren't you?'

'Is there any use me being here?'

'I don't know. How much am I part of him?'

Early on I learned Dee's knack for saying something that stops a conversation in its tracks.

◆

She liked to talk about the valley, the place, the topography, as if she were locating herself by constructing the province with her voice. Later that night, by candlelight, she had pulled out a map and, with her finger, led me down the tiny winding roads to the quiet shore towns. My eyes flitted back and forth between her long fingers and the map beneath them. She swirled the pad of her forefinger over the areas that were farmland and swept her nails over the woodland. Her palm became the heady south wind that rolled over the bay from the Vermont forests.

We sat together in the kitchen. A sweet, heavy aroma had sunk into my clothes. The dim light of the candles strained my eyes until they watered.

I looked around for signs of Henry but there were none. She had moved out soon after Henry's suicide so he was never here, but I thought there would be more traces of him here: his presence, his possessions, his imprint.

'Why did you leave Toronto, Dee?'

'I've wanted to leave for a long time. A long time.' Was she thinking about him now? 'It seems like a big change in my life but it's not. It's not. And I wasn't suddenly free to come here. It was just time, that's all. My writing was getting clouded by the city, claustrophobic, landlocked. The novel I'm working on needs space, grandeur and a certain amount of self-imposed isolation.'

I could sense her locking up. Or drifting away. 'Know what you mean. I admire you out here. I'm envious.'

She smiled out the window. She knew I was sucking up, but tried not to let me know she knew. 'It's late, there's two empty bedrooms upstairs if you want to stay, and,' she paused as if reconsidering, 'since we all know creativity is work, you can stay as long as you want if you pitch in and help with the chores.'

'Thank you … and the film thanks you.'

She got up to go to bed, turned at the door. 'Don't get me wrong, I want this film to be good, I really do, and I think it will be good. He told me you might come to talk to me.' Pause. 'I just don't like being a pawn in someone else's plan.' Pause. Then, from up the stairwell, 'We'll work it out.'

◆

We knelt together in the sandy soil picking beetles from the broccoli leaves. It was midsummer and the broccoli heads were getting large, nearly the hand's width they needed to be for picking. Dee picked them and kept them in a cold storage room in the back of the barn until retailers came to buy them.

The black and yellow beetles were on every second leaf, it seemed, and my thumb got sore and stained black from snicking the life out of them. Even though it was hot and there was hardly any breeze, Dee had on thick grey socks under her hiking boots. Her legs were tanned brown and unshaven with scabs and scuffs on her knees. She worked mechanically, muffled in her own thoughts, and my jerky attempts at conversation only seemed to intrude.

She would not speak of him.

The work filled my body up with a fiery liquid surge that I had not felt for a long time. Dirt, green plant juice, mosquitoes in my teeth, the sun drying out the mushroom moistness of my skin. A gravel road ran along the market-garden field opposite the old house. Occasionally, a half-ton would rumble down it, sending up a spume of dust that drifted across the field to us. Next to the broccoli, a large strawberry patch sang, calling us over once in a while for a red slap on the tongue. In the stillest part of the afternoon, you could hear the surf down the hills from Wolfville by Grand Pré. The world was not about change anymore, the surf and progress, it was about shifting essences, diffusion, the subtle turns of illusion which make us see the illusion's trick.

I decided to try and get Dee to help me with the film. Henry wouldn't approve, but he was dead. There was something here about to create itself.

She caught me daydreaming and hucked a big broccoli head into my belly with a thud. 'When we're done here, there's wire fence to mend down by the pond.' And then, under her breath, ' … city boy.'

♦

On the third night she rolled a joint and lit it as we sat on the couch in the living room. I had taken a nap on the couch the day before (it was clear I wasn't used to the work but wasn't going to admit that) and it cradled me so deftly that I was asleep in seconds. I wiggled down into its arms and watched her lean over the paper meticulously. Everything seemed dreamlike, fuzzy like in an old movie. I started to tell her about what I was thinking for the film. I wanted to start with some black-and-white shots of where he hung out on College and around his house with a voice-over reading some of his poems about place and the city but then I thought that might be too conventional. I tried to imagine a more direct depiction of his death, something dramatic but honest. As I mused she nodded and blew smoke up towards a hole in the roof. She passed it over and I took a drag while thinking about why I was worried about 'honesty.' It tasted sweet and rich. I felt my body relaxing as finally I was able to start telling someone about my project. She was a good listener; often she raised an eyebrow, turned a glance, nodded, frowned, tsked, all those reactions that let you know someone is out there at the other end of the sound waves randomly issuing from your mouth. When she was looking away I found myself thinking about the idea of a muse. Could those eighteenth-century poets mean this when they wrote about muses?

Dee's voice sparked up and flashed through my haze. 'Honesty is the last thing you need, honey. If you're going to do this out of obligation to … him, then you have to resist the temptation to just dump him in a box. Artists want to be responded to artistically. You know that.'

I was scolded. I wanted to move closer to her on the couch. Of course, I would have to be more creative. Henry would not fit into the conventional documentary biography. His texts wouldn't allow it. I wanted to write something to Dee, though. I moved closer to her on the couch.

About an hour into our conversation, she looked directly at me. We were sitting close and both comfortably high. I was not used to the syrupy warmth of the smoke in my chest and surprised myself with an erection against my forearm. Soon after (although time was syrupy, too) she looked directly at me. Not directly like she had before but more piercing, to get my fluid attention. 'Ambitious filmmaker studies brilliant dead writer, learns his life, his philosophy, his intellectual dramas, his weaknesses, takes his lover as his own.' She paused. 'No. It's a bad script, kid. It's old, it's cliché, it's too easy. It won't play. Find something new.'

She looked away, took a long drag, exhaled towards the roof.

She was right. I would have to start again.

♦

Beginnings were always a tentative time for Dee. I learned I had to start conversations on a certain note, a certain slant, a careful and gentle opening up of things. Most of my attempts at broaching subjects had fallen dead on the spot. But I learned more and more how to ease into something, catching Dee's attention. I had to catch her attention with language. It was an insistent pressure, this demand she placed on my mouth.

'What is your name short for? Dee, it is short for something?'

'It is short for me. All names are short for something else.' She had obviously been thinking about this more than I had. 'No, it's just Dee. He used to make fun of it, call me D without the *eeee* sound. Just *D, duh*. So often things he said were turned into the past tense when he included my name at the end. "I love the way things sound D." The jerk.' She realized she was talking about him, shot me an angry look. I hadn't tried to trick her. She went silent for a long time.

'What's yours short for? Jason?'

'No, no, it's just Jay, like the bird. Funny we both have letters as names – or letter sounds as names anyway.'

'Think we're elemental? Maybe there's twenty-six of us out there, all with names that are letters of the alphabet. Wish I was H. But then how do you spell that? Hate to be W. Whew. What was his favourite colour?' She tossed the ball into my court suddenly.

'No colour at all.'

She nodded as if I had gotten it right. 'I have some papers. I'll dig them out tomorrow. A vow is a vow, but I'll help.'

This testing might have been devastating if I hadn't been desperate already. Dee could do what she wished with me; I was at her mercy. And, somehow, that was comforting.

♦

Henry was a Minke whale whose song (a faint memory of a blue burgeoning love) echoed, shuddered in from the coast. He surfaced, blew, submerged into the depths again without a trace. The ocean refuses nothing.

On a Sunday deep in the grip of dry heat, we stood next to my tripod as I filmed passing whales near Yarmouth. A handful of crumpled Nova Scotia maps rested on the car seat behind us. Dee went along with my wandering search. Pilot whales dipped by. Two Minke whales started me dreaming of deluge, being submerged. I waited for something bigger. Gulls and terns whipped up the buffer of air that collected and flew from the water. We stood eating the tuna sandwiches we had packed and watched, either through the lens or not. Our hair wanted to be part of the surf. Dee finally asked me, 'And what do whales have to do with your film?' Hmmm, she had me there. I shrugged and said, 'I don't know, I'm sort of letting go here. Getting lost instead of mapping.' She looked down the coast-line without comment for a while. She leaned over and looked through the camera lens. 'Yeah, me too.'

♦

'Sometimes life can leave a human body like speech. Clear, resonant – a series of notes constructed with all the air of the lungs. Expended. Exhaled. Expired. A demand for response; for the next word, for wailing, for monuments. The word 'soul' leaves the dying mouth in a profound ellipsis, leaving the reader to sound out its enigmatic syllables. Death, just beyond life, becomes a rapturous narrative frame, a place of enunciation which the reader translates clumsily, translates knowing the translation is incomplete, translates aware that nuances are being lost, that depth is being shored up in the process. The act of deciphering necessarily fails — necessarily fails because of the imprecision of living. The city of the dead welcomes the newcomers like national poets, like philosopher kings and queens. And the dead look back over their shoulders and utter a truth from the other side, a token tossed back through a closing door, an image coalescing past the last sentence. The reader can fill in that space only by extrapolation, fill it in with their own inexpressible 'not-life,' complete the sign with exuberant speculations and fears. The death-grip of ideas grasps us with the shadowy hands of poetry, the 'not-being' in the spaces between words holding us fascinated and unsatisfied.'

I tapped off the camera remote with my foot. Where had that come from? Dee turned the corner into my room, eyes wide. She had overheard. She just stood there staring for a long time. 'Print it,' she finally said and walked away.

♦

She liked to talk about her work, not to show off but to hear it aloud, test the text out. She was in the middle of a novel about Catherine the Great from the point of view of a male lover. Walking by her bedroom I saw stacks of manuscript on her small desk and the floor beside it, stacks that teetered because of their height.

She asked, 'What status do you think that male lover had in court? He was a military man. Would he be honoured? Joked about? Would he be afraid for his life?'

I thought for a moment. 'Probably nervous most of all – a lot of men would want to be in his shoes, would want to knock him off.'

'Not only from rivals but from her hand as well. She killed more than one man.' She looked over at me, looked me up and down. 'Would you like to have been Catherine's lover?'

I stuttered a bit, 'Sure, sure, exciting … life to lead.'

She grinned, either mocking or pleased. 'What do you think Catherine's favourite dinner was?'

She knew that one but wouldn't tell me. 'Catherine was not the master of her destiny but neither was she a cog in the machine. She was, I'd hazard to guess, untraceable. Biographers tried, but what crap! Pitiful attempts to create her. Pitiful and desperate. That is what first intrigued me – the fact that so many had tried, like she was a prize every man tried to pin down and fuck for all she was worth. She's not there – not in those flimsy attempts at drama. She's long gone. The trick is not to even try to catch her.'

I began wondering if Dee was using me as research for her novel just as much as I was using her as research for my film.

She pulled out a few pages and read.

♦

Reign

I regarded Peter III for the first time on the drilling field. At the time, I had met Ekaterina only twice and only the faintest flickerings of her attention were emerging. You see how even my memory of Peter is entirely contingent on her; he hinges on my thoughts of her, as does everything.

Rumour from Alexeev in the kitchen held that Ekaterina was already fostering 'favourites' in the court and that she and Peter had come to an agreement about courtly lovers. I had heard all kinds of reports of his immature obsession with little war toys and mock battles on papier mâché, his rampant anti-Russian sentiments (I would have no king who did not love the country he ruled!), and his reputation for being profoundly impotent. This latter interested me most since Ekaterina's early indication was that she certainly was not. She instantly held a sexual presence in the court; her mannerisms, her glances, her unbridled laughter beckoned attention. Her courtier, Praskov'ia Bruce, had felt me out (and by this I mean literally) and inquired into my impressions of the Empress. I had already felt like I had been summoned by her – was there any choice?

Out in the courtyard, Peter looked pale, like he had been bled recently. My Guards, recently from the wars in Prussia, were behind me. They stood at attention for him but I could sense their tension, see it in the set of their shoulders, the purse of their lips. He was mounted and shouting in a high-pitched tenor at his men on the opposite side of the court. They were all dressed in pressed Prussian-style uniforms. A ripple of hushed curses began flowing through my men and the two small armies regarded each other across Golitsyn Square. I hoped Ekaterina was watching.

Even here, in my confounded prison, I hope Ekaterina is watching.

♦

The next day, back in the rows of broccoli plants, I nudged Dee towards talking more about Henry. Finally she turned to me. 'Look, I cannot tell you who he was. You have everything you need already. I am here, you have his writing, you are here. Don't think about it so much, just do it. Don't make the film, let the film happen. Just stay lost.'

She paused, looking straight at me. I noticed she had bigger shoulders than me. She turned back to her work. 'I won't rewrite what he's done himself – not that plain, not that obvious. One thing, though; I would have killed him if he hadn't done it himself.' She allowed herself a brief smile at the broccoli head as it popped off into her hand.

At that moment, at the sight of that brief expression on her face, I realized I had been desperate to turn her into a dangerous woman. Broccolis don't have 'heads.' The dead bird by the door. I was intimidated, yes. She was physically imposing, yes. But she moved through her day with grace and gentleness, not with malice and mystery.

The film threatened to become about her, not Henry.

The mystery was of my making; the malice came from my insecurity.

The film threatened to become about me.

I didn't seem to think it a problem.

♦

The morning I told her my conundrum over the rented car, she suggested a trip. I had been nervous about the safety of the car in her driveway — it seemed like the country road was a tough farmboy waiting to scratch its gleaming finish again. Even she seemed like a coarse surface next to the sheer lines of its hood.

As it was, I was paying for the car to sit so I agreed to the idea of the trip. She got out maps and pointed immediately to the top of the long strip of Nova Scotia. There. Her fingernail fit snug in a bay called Meat Cove. There, she said. I mouthed the place, an invocation of the printed name. Meat Cove.

As we packed she told me the story of the cove as she had heard it through some of the local townspeople. Shouting from her room, she said it got its name because it was a docking place for ships picking up moose meat. Hundreds upon thousands of moose carcasses were hauled to the sheltered pier to be loaded on ships headed for the States and Europe. This was hardly attractive to me but she assured me that people said it was magnificent. Trust me, she said, standing at my bedroom door, flushed and excited, a duffel bag slung over her shoulder.

◆

The trip ended up taking six days, most of them in silence. The wind was high, especially along the shore, and the car bucked and dipped against it. Dee sat with her feet on the dash staring up at the wild-eyed sky and the high skittish clouds. Our conversations in the car were hardly remarkable, but the pace, the fits and starts of ideas, formed a quiet rhythm. One would start, 'Did you ever wonder why ...' the other would pause and then reply, 'I dunno, I guess ...' and nothing was ever decided. We bumped heads over a few things; she couldn't believe I was a member of the Communist Party, called it silly and even pretentious. I asked her about her money, how she got it since it was obvious she wasn't going to live off broccoli.

She asked about my parents and childhood and I answered freely, not feeling at all like she might be psychoanalyzing me. I started telling Dee everything, everything. I went on and on about my family and problems.

I grew up on a farm near Baytree, Alberta – a town name I always liked because 'baytree' is another name for laurel, which is associated with such things as 'poet laureate' even though I never did become a poet like I thought I would. My parents – and I had always just said this plainly when people asked – were both killed in a house fire when I was young. An aunt, Aunt Gwen, and a friend named Apology stayed with me until I was sixteen and could run the farm on my own. I felt that I was well-loved by my extended family: Gwen, cousins, grandparents who lived near Spirit River. The town, too, though sometimes suspicious of my solitary and eccentric ways, was generally supportive.

I had some trouble with delusions – maybe because of my parents' deaths – in which I would talk to the devil. It seemed very real, it still seems real. It was a crisis of faith. Maybe someday I will make a film about it. But I finished high school with good marks and went to university in the city. Film came late, only after I bounced around in Education Departments, where I thought I might teach high school, and English, where I thought I might write poetry.

Dee was watching me and I felt compelled to slow down.

'I feel like, in a way, the death of my parents taught me something.'

I stopped.

'Death teaches us something?' Now it was her turn to be tentative.

She kept her eyes on the road.

'It is something we learn. Up here.' I pointed to my head. 'And here,' palm over my stomach. 'I used to have nightmares about hell but then I realized it was our house burning. I don't anymore. That's not death. Death is about the limits, or maybe the limitlessness, of flesh. All the manifestations of my parents were strung out in me. That is what I learned.'

'Is there a difference between haunting and knowledge?'

◆

We stopped at a pebbly beach near Wreck Cove where a small stream ran over mossy stones and the sandy cliffs jutted to the water's edge. We took off our sandals and waded partway into the water. The water surged up our legs and the cold slapped into our calves like a cramp. We waded further, up to our thighs. We stopped, standing there in the ocean, many arm lengths apart. There seemed to be a drop-off not far in front of us and we could feel the beginnings of an undertow tugging at our knees. In books, this would be an important juncture in the story. We stood, several arm lengths apart, looking out at the ocean, the rolling waves, the sky swooping up from them. In books, this would be a beginning, a transition between the old and the new, a change of mediums, the solid ground to chaotic water. We stood, looking out at the ocean, a few arm lengths apart, the sky swooping up from the slow, ceaseless motion of the world.

♦

Henry. H-e-n-r-y. Why? The letters jumped off the page every time I ran across them. Henry is ... Henry was ... Henry said ... I did not know what tense to use.

His name became synonymous with fleeting images, a face, fragments of poetry and the indomitable anger of Dee. The last was not consistent – Dee, too, eluded my impulse to capture character, compose drama. She cut me off at every narrative turn, remained, at best, inconsistent. Her refusal to say his name remained a gap in my understanding of him.

Lines from Henry's 1994 poem called 'Devotional':

> *text holds death in the next*
> *word, carousel, the will to*
> *not say the very things*
> *we most desire, remaining*
> *an afterimage, a glimpse, a mystery –*
> *a secret, secreting the urge to say again, again*
> *without end*

The more I read his poems, the more I saw his suicide as a culmination of his work. Not a sacrifice, not melodrama – more a refusal, a poetic gesture to read, just like the last lines of many of his poems. A poem shouldn't be comparable to a life, should it? But what if? What if writing and life aren't that different? What if the thing we call language is as vibrant and full as a human life? The Adamic text.

The rough asphalt shook the car, jiggling the print, and I stopped reading before I got a headache.

We stopped for the night at the North 'A' Motel near Sydney. The pub next to the motel closed early but the bartender sold us a twenty-four of rye to get us through. Not that we'd drink that much, but that was the image we wanted to give the bartender. In reality, neither of us could hold our liquor very well and we usually stopped after two or three, knowing the repercussions of drinking more. We watched TV instead. Neither of us watched much at home; I had one but usually rented films to watch late at night, and Dee didn't even own one. Kids must have had to radically adjust when they visited her place. Did kids ever visit?

'Why did you and Henry never have kids?' I could be blunter now – I was not in her house where I could easily be thrown out, and she had committed to a trip in my car. This question verged on being about Henry. It was on the line. I watched the Bugs Bunny episode intently, waiting for an answer.

'I was pregnant when he died.'

Ooof. I could not look at her. My stomach clenched and I felt like I might hyperventilate. Pregnant. When he died.

'He didn't know.'

That did not mean anything to me until later, upon reflection.

'I lost in it the seventh week – it wasn't "viable."' She said 'viable' as if it wasn't her word. 'Don't be shocked, it happens. It's actually my second miscarriage. Both times I lost them before I really knew I had them. Can't see myself as a mom anyway.'

There was no remorse in her voice at all, which startled me a little. Her apparent lack of emotion seemed very unwomanly. Or maybe she was putting on an act.

I had to think what I meant by 'womanly.'

♦

Meat Cove met us at the bottom of our stomachs and the backs of our throats. Wind and vertigo met us at the brink of annihilation. The car stopped a few metres from the cliff edge. We got out, feeling the wind suck and push as it corkscrewed out of the tight, high cliff faces of the cove.

Cape Breton had launched into a new stratosphere of air: salt-soaked, wet, filled with the discomfort of land meeting sky meeting sea. And us.

We knew as we looked north from our cliff perch that Newfoundland sat somewhere just over the horizon. But leaning to the east it was hard not to feel the expanse, the weight of ocean as it churned and turned and rolled. Visions of Iceland, Norwegian fjords, the ice-locked Arctic Ocean glimmered somewhere in the Atlantic surf.

We were at the end, the last stop, the final destination. Unless you were a seal or a bird or a fisherman, this was as far as you went. It seemed like a leaping-off point into oblivion.

This, I thought, was where Henry was.

Dee took a step closer to the edge and I followed. We were close enough to see the thin strand of rocks piled up against the bottom of the cliff. Close enough to imagine the spinning descent to those rocks. At the same time it was hard not to imagine a gust of wind strong enough to push us out over the water so that we would land in the ocean's arms, breathless and safe.

Dee took another step forward. I followed. Any more and we would be lost. The vertigo and the weight of air were calling us. Pebbles fell free and bounced soundlessly down the cliff face. Earth turned insubstantial.

Dee turned to me and said, 'Let's go.'

I looked into her eyes – burgundy in the green-grey light – looked to see what she was saying. What was she saying?

'Let's go. Off. Out.'

What was she? Was she? Off?

'Let's do it. For Henry. One more step to find out what he knows.'

Her voice gusted in swells against my averted face. The water below shimmered and the waves seemed tiny eddies of thought. They moved in and then bounced back out, flopping and butting into each other.

'This is the place Henry found. The edge where you can step back or step forward. Can you really tell his story without following him there? He is what waits if we go off. He is there. Let's go.'

I looked around to see if anyone was watching. Her voice crackled through my paralysis – I doubted I could move forward or back at that moment. How would I finish my film if I were dead? Would the company finish it? Probably not. What had I left behind – enough to make a complete film? Patchy at best. It would not flow together very well, though it might come across as some kind of postmodern collage. What about the car? I hadn't paid for it. Was this a lovers' leap?

Dee watched me. I was in her wind. I could not tell if she was serious or testing me. Such is the nature of a test, I guess.

I wanted to say yes.

It was not a matter of not having a good life. It was not a matter of being depressed or despairing about the world. It was about curiosity, about art, about something human which has been beyond our reach, hovering there, just out of reach, off the edge.

Even more than that, it was about Dee.

I did not know if she was serious or not. I did not know what she meant when she said 'Let's go.' She was unreadable, perched there, suspended over the transient water of Meat Cove, above the ocean that would accept us unconditionally.

'Let's go,' she said. I waited for my own answer.

♦

QUICK FADE-IN to wide-angle view of South Mountains and fields. MALE VOICE-OVER begins:

> I am thinking about nothing but the ways in
> which two people might connect over time.
> This poem met me there.

PAUSE

> *Anticipation*

PAUSE

the moth invented the flame
drew in its flicker
breathing its perfume
wings like lungs

the moth invented the flame
became a brush to paint shadows
a lover darting huge
against the ceiling, walls of possibility

the moth invented the flame
to distort the terrifying blue
the rows of clean white birch
the screen door gleaming like teeth

the moth invented the flame
and a leaping cocoon dream
candlestick wax wrapped
melting into a nimble tip

the moth invented the flame
like a lily from heaven
its curves and sweet sanctum
divulged, incense and ash

the moth invented the flame
to mock the butterfly glamour
the monarch so virtuous and clean
their hidden orgies an inferno

the moth invented the flame
the end the story, one last scene
with dazzle and flare
and a tense lingering smell

a scent you still remember
every time you fall in love

SOUND OF RUSTLING PAPER and a quiet SIGH. STILL on landscape for three seconds and QUICK FADE-OUT TO BLACK.

♦

I told her of the traces of Henry I saw. I saw ashes in her eyes.

♦

'Here, pretend I am … him.'

Dee was somewhere on the other side of a lilac hedge that was frosted over with purple-tinged white blooms. The scent was like chilled drambuie.

'Pretend I am him and ask me questions – anything you want to know.' Dee was in one of her generous moods; I knew I had to take advantage of these times before she turned again. She was a voice emanating from the foliage.

'Are you in love with Dee?' Shit, should've waited with that one. Was she going to balk now?

'Absolutely. Irrevocably. Undeniably. Love in the grandest tradition. Love like the kind inscribed in stone by Egyptian pharaohs. Love like a plague. Love like in poems.' She stopped. I dared not speak.

She was Dee again. 'He has ... had a lover in Mexico. Well, she still was his lover, still is the lover even though he isn't doing any lovin' nowadays.' She snorted as if at a private joke. 'She is a violinist and has a house on a cliff on the ocean. He didn't know I knew.'

I wondered if she knew about the lover in High Park.

'I heard through another poet who had gone to the World Poetry Conference in 1995 who told a bookstore owner who sleeps with someone in his department who told me out of spite. Bastard. But it was good to know – at least it explained some of his behaviour that was annoying me. And why he adored that ugly little country villa so much. And the significance of his claim that the Mexicans loved poets. Not like here in Canada where they are treated like psychos.'

'Have you ever thought of leaving Canada if it is so bad?'

'I'm not a poet ... or at least don't call myself a poet. Novelists are second-class citizens but not as bad off as poets.'

'Your writing is very poetic, though.'

'Her name was ... is Luisa Guererro. She, supposedly, is magic. You should go see her. She would have seen parts of ... him I never did.'

I couldn't tell if she was being sarcastic, bitter or melancholy. I heard her walk away from the hedge.

◆

'Let's talk about arts funding.' I almost included the word 'then' petulantly at the end of my statement. I was frustrated at her silence. I had told myself not to get frustrated and she would come around but I found myself frustrated. 'Do you think the arts should get government funding?'

She finally looked over at me incredulously. 'You really want to get into this?'

'Yeah – let's go.' I grinned.

This produced a smile, too. 'Okay, well, it's like welfare in some ways. It's needed but I think it'd be more important to address why it is needed. Take, for example, your film. You have a grant ... maybe.

'Ten thousand dollars over eight months – plus reasonable expenses.' Ah, and I had just managed to forget about the car.

'Ten grand of government money to produce a documentary that will not make it to even fringe theatres, will sit in the NFB archives, will be purchased for four hundred dollars each by five universities. It will be lucky to get a press release and a small poster. Meanwhile, a thirty-million-dollar Hollywood movie gets advertisements in papers and TV every day and is sold out for several-week runs across the city. Replace me with Danielle Steel and you have the same scenario. Now, the problem lies in what people buy. Hollywood films entertain. Your film? Your film will confuse, frustrate. Only people with film degrees will enjoy it. Only people with English degrees enjoy my novels. So, what we need to do is give everyone film and English degrees. Everyone.'

'Sounds like a Catherine the Great edict. She was a big patron of the arts, wasn't ... '

She glared at me. 'I am not Catherine the Great. She is a character in my novel. I am a real live person. Got it?'

◆

Henry was a ghost writer for at least three celebrities – a retired hockey player, a former premier of Alberta and a British actor who didn't want the British press to track down the real writer so he hired a Canadian. He detested the work but was able to finance his trips via these droll books. Autobiography scared him. He didn't mind the grandiose nature of it, he didn't even mind the politics and back-stabbing – it was the honesty that bothered him. It was those points in the autobiographies where the clients wanted to really say something they had been holding back, the secrets and confessions, that really bothered him. He delighted in being someone else but not when it was too real.

In one of the autobiographies, there is a strange tangential passage that got by the editors. It is a rumination on memory and is an obvious departure from the tenor of the book. I think Henry wrote it in deliberately because he wanted to assert himself into the flimsy construction of the book. An autobiography written by a ghost writer. I am sure he shuddered at the thought. He probably was also tickled by the absurdity of the thing. The passage plays with the idea, the hypocrisy of text:

If I may, I would like to pause in this headlong tracery of a lifelong journey's path to comment briefly on the process by which I have recollected this quest. These accounts are myths of my own making. In other words, a life does not equal an autobiography. Even more than that, memory as an intermediary adds another level of separation. So you have a life, memory of that life, and then a written translation of that memory into text. Even more than that, I may not be who you think I am when I am writing of my life. I am not the same as I was yesterday or last year. It is like filming

another film playing on a screen that is on a moving vehicle while you are
mounted in a separate moving vehicle. Can you visualize that? Two flatbed
trucks careening across a flat plain, one showing a film, the other filming
while swerving and speeding alongside. It is an experiment in physics, a
physics of perspective and representation. The images, the facts of the
subject are clearly secondary to the idea of re-creation, the speed, the blur,
the ghostly images that spiral off the page.

♦

I asked Dee whether she had ever ghost written a book.

'I ghost wrote one of his books of poetry – can you guess which one?'

She wasn't trying to destroy me but she certainly felt it was her duty to destabilize my world. Often her revelations or proclamations came first thing in the morning so she could jolt me out of my coffee-soothed grog.

'It was a lark – a bet, actually. He challenged me to imitate his poetry so seamlessly that his editors wouldn't notice. It was easy, really; I just had to be more pretentious and elusive. I studied his line-break principles, his diction, his punctuation quirks. I traced his thematic trends and his methods of coming up with titles. All of his last lines come across as questions.' She paused. 'I mention this because I am wondering if I shouldn't produce another "ghost manuscript," you know, unpublished poems I've dug up from his files – every writer has them. It's what's done when a famous poet dies.' She turned to face me fully across the kitchen table. 'Would you like to help me write it?'

She loved to be overwhelming, a rogue wave to sweep me off my shoreline perch.

Not looking at me, she said, presumably quoting someone, 'I am resolved, as you know, to perish or to reign.'

We sat down at the kitchen table to write. The fat cat flopped in my lap and snored.

'Okay, first lines ... '

> the most ghostly writing could take
> a whole afternoon to enter my veins

'Your turn.' Dee slid the looseleaf page over to me. She was serious.

'Well, I am not much of a poet.' She tsked and knocked the table twice with her index finger. I looked at the lines she had written. 'He liked the iterative,' I said, 'so can we make this ... ' I crossed out 'could take' so it read

> the most ghostly writing taking
> a whole afternoon to enter my veins

and then quickly wrote

> as if my body were actual
> and the phantasmal less torturous, less eternal

I slid the page back. I was holding my breath.

Dee leaned far over the page. She held the pencil oddly, with all of her fingers touching the shaft. It made it look like she was engraving, chiselling away at stone. She added a dash to the end of my last line and then

I know I am alive because my imaginary
heart is beating, and love

I thought I saw a shadow pass across the window above the sink.
Dee looked, too. The page was in front of me.

love spreads up through clay and loam,
tendrils of the repressed, a claim on history

Pass. A cock crowed.

to revise beginning, revise why narration
stays close, a neural track around my house

Pass. An added period.

but my house is not one, that fiction
eroding into rivulets, streams, rivers of potential

Pass.

which I draw on, suck into my belly
until I am drunk
unfermented and expectorating back
into travel, travelling
merely departed, parting the lush
juncture of here and not
here, cries another word, stay,
but the word is synonymous with

death, the one I know will rewrite
the word, death
rewriting the word rewriting.

III

Jay

In the morning I decided to fly to Mexico to speak with Henry's lover. His other lover. Ex-lover.

It was entirely unlike me. I had never been anywhere and here I was jetting off on a whim to do peripheral research (at best) with a contact who may not be around. It was the one place outside Canada where I had a lead, a contact, a place to stay (being practical), and a chance to find out aspects of Henry that Dee did not know. The budget couldn't handle the whole thing so I'd have to cover a bunch of it from my own pocket. I took a charter flight out of Halifax to Toronto and then directly to Acapulco. From there, a ferry was to take me down the coast to Salina Cruz in Oaxaca. That's where his villa was, just outside town. Dee had pictures. The tan clay walls of the small adobe house gave way to towering hills and an impossibly green sea.

Seeing Henry in one of the pictures with a loose-fitting shirt and sandals, I couldn't help but think of Neruda. But Henry was not Neruda.

I had no idea what I would find in Mexico, but I had to do something to shake the stunning lack of progress on my documentary.

My leaving had other motivations. The fact was Dee threatened to engulf me completely. If I was going to finish this documentary, if I was going to get the last part of my grant money, I needed to get some space. It was only practical. I had to make at least a gesture towards Henry's biography.

In my last-minute packing, I stuffed the draft of *Reign* Dee had given me to read on the plane. The space of her novel, Catherine, Gregorii, jostled inside my film – I could not resist. Even before the plane had lifted off from the bumpy Halifax runway, I had wrestled the manuscript out of my carry-on and was diving in.

♦

Reign

If I remember correctly, she arrived at court on a blustery Wednesday and she looked at everyone, each individual courtier, as if we were all potential lovers. We collectively blushed at her gaze. At the time, I was merely an above-average soldier, a lowly captain with no political aspirations at all. But that look – it was a look that said, 'I can make you something else. Come to me.'

Her new name, we had been told, was Ekaterina Alexeena. Lofty, indeed! Her former name, the one left behind in Anhalt-Zerbst, was said to be Sophia. I vowed to remember that name since it is the one that seemed to carry the sound of her on its lips. *Sophia*. I mouthed it when I saw her enter a room or stride out to the stables. I do not easily fall into the thralls of love, but this queen captured my attention in every way. Easily.

She was to marry the snivelling Peter and we all pitied her before we even saw her. A sacrificial lamb, it seemed to us. The political balance had been shuffled and the court was having to adjust to the idea of this foreign princess alongside a foreign future king. Russian patriots were banding, looking to me for direction. My brother's gaze across the court today said it all – he was at his boiling point. Was this future queen going to stall our plans? Save us?

I remember that it was a Wednesday when she came simply because the banquet planned for Ekaterina's arrival interrupted the normal schedule of the kitchen. This was notable because normally on a Wednesday Martina took over from Josef's stern rule and made her spine-tingling cucumber trout. I never missed a Wednesday meal in the palace. My stomach was my political motivation. I admit it. I am not one to puff up my conduct or hide my desires. I am what I am. The royal kitchen was my haunt – the three huge stoves and echoing stone cistern were as familiar to me as the host of cooks who worked there. And the trout, that was my desire.

1 whole trout, weighing approx. 1.5 kg
Per litre water:
  2 tbs. salt
  1 bay leaf
  8 peppercorns
  1 slice of lemon
1/2 cup powdered aspic
2 fresh cucumbers
5 dl water or fish stock
Garnish: parsley, fresh dill and lemon slices

Choose a saucepan that will hold the fish bent into a semi-circle. Place the fish with the backbone uppermost in the pan, just cover with water, and add the flavourings. Bring to the boil and skim. A 1–1.5 kg trout should simmer for 5 minutes. A 1.5–2.5 kg trout should simmer for 8 minutes. A 2.5–3 kg trout should simmer for 10 minutes. Remove the saucepan from the heat and leave the fish in the stock until it is cold, preferably until it is to be served. It can be kept like this for up to a day in an ice box. Dissolve the aspic in the water. Remove the fish from the stock and cut along the back fins, around the tail and around the head. Pull the skin carefully off the body, leaving it on the tail and head. Remove the strip of fat along the back fins. Let the fish drain before placing it on a serving dish. When the aspic begins to thicken, brush it on the fish and place the cucumber slices like scales over the aspic. Be sure to cover the whole fish, as this will prevent it from becoming dry. Garnish with lemon slices, parsley and fresh dill.

Gregorii Orlov is my name and I may go down in history as Ekaterina's most famous lover, but my god, that trout should be remembered, too!

I leaned forward and looked down the table at Her Majesty and knew I would follow her, like a hunger, anywhere.

♦

We were airborne and the novel drew me in. Being unearthed was what I needed. I licked my lips.

♦

But Mexico was still very much a part of the earth. Salina Cruz greeted me with the whispers of him. It was late October, and the air was hot and damp. Henry's empty villa was on the ocean side of town and was close to Luisa's house. Bougainvilleas climbed up the portcullis that opened onto the gravel street, and vines fell over the veranda and courtyard which was full of trespassing kids when I arrived. They scattered with shrieks and haughty jeers, and I was left standing in the riotous green with fig and pineapple rinds under my sandals. The look the eldest boy, the one who left last, gave me was one that seemed to say, what right do you have to be here? why are you here at all?

Or maybe I was projecting.

I slept on a bare box spring with a musty blue blanket thrown over it. Large lumbering beetles and suspicious lime-green anole lizards reluctantly gave up the space. The first day I nearly drowned in the light – the sun cracked my irises like nutshells and left my pupils bare, wet and tender. I longed for shadow.

When I finally ventured out from the villa it was to fulfill basic needs: to find food and to find Luisa. Down the hill ran a gravel track lined graciously with tall slender palms. They seemed young and gregarious, unlike the palms by the coast which seemed like artifacts, staged and tacky. It was odd that there weren't more new trees like this. Partway down the hill I passed by a pen of pigs that had been empty on my way up. Eight or ten pigs grubbed under the sod in the shade, casting curious glances my way as I passed.

I was suddenly ecstatic. I felt like the world was reborn. There seemed to be no reason for this sudden surge.

Dee's directions were vague, but I knew I could just ask around and it wouldn't be hard to find Luisa. She worked for a local paper in a nearby town so I figured she might not be at home during the day. I had tried not to construct her in my imagination too much on the way. Living with Dee had made me come to realize how much of my knowing had become known before real knowing was even possible. I liked to surround myself with ideas of security – even if those ideas were pure fantasy.

Luisa was not going to be my fantasy.

The small town was called both Salina Cruz and Salina María, depending on who you asked. It seemed to have something to do with Christian and non-Christian sentiments but wasn't consistent even on those lines. The main street ran parallel to the sea and was much like a stereotypical Hollywood set for a Western – false fronts and boardwalks. No saloon, as far as I could see, though.

The street address Dee had dug up was 4 Callejón Coatlicue and she said she thought it ran off the main street. It looked like everything ran from the central *zócalo* anyway. There weren't many people about – it was a Tuesday, I think. Café patrons watched as I squinted at the few signs posted around the *zócalo*. A tired-looking statue sat over a tepid pool of water in the centre. I finally stopped to ask a shopkeeper and she pointed to an unmarked alley on the north side. I counted doors as I walked into the shade. The fourth was up a flight of iron-grate stairs. When I reached the top of the swaying apparatus I knocked on a freshly painted bright yellow door. It was only then I became fully nervous. There was a bell to the side of the door and I rang it after waiting a minute. It clanged louder than I expected and I quickly grabbed it to stop the din. I heard movement behind the door.

She opened the door wide immediately and smiled a warm, unconditional greeting. This was startling. What if I intended no good? 'Come in, entra, por favor!' She turned with a wave and disappeared into the apartment.

'You are Luisa, yes?' I called after her. 'Si, si.' I had to stoop slightly to get in the door and stood waiting at the entrance for her to reappear. She called from the other room, 'Come in, venga pronto!' I poked my head around the corner into a living room with four enormous tan leather couches circling a glass table. A small black and white TV was on but silent in one of the window sills. The picture barely showed because of the glare. Luisa was pouring drinks out of a pitcher filled with ice. She tossed a sprig of leaves in the bottom of the glass.

'To cool you off, señor – you know this drink, no? All Americans like it, I think. Hemingway, you know. Come and sit.' She beckoned to the couch. She was a striking woman with a strong nose and high forehead. She had a red kerchief over her hair and ink stains on her hands.

She watched as I set my camera bag on the couch between us. 'You are American or Canadian, my friend?'

'Oh, Canadian. I come from Toronto to ask you about a writer named Henry Black.' I shifted to see her face when I said the name. She smiled and nodded.

'Si, it is a shame his dying. What is your name, young prince?'

'Jay … not the letter … J-A-Y. Jay … '

'A pretty name,' she interrupted, 'and you are come to find out why Henry killed himself?'

'How did you hear that he … ?'

'Inevitable. It was where his path led. He told me he would – not directly but in his poems, in his ideas – as his final statement. "Grito," you might say, eh? Besides, I was invited to the funeral. I didn't go but it was nice to be invited. Here, you drink. Have you had lunch?'

'Yes,' I lied, thinking she might not have much.

'You're lying. I will get you something. Drink, drink.' She seemed almost angry. She got up and went through another door into a lime-green kitchen. Her voice rang back into the living room. 'Henry said you might come some day. You see, he had everything in order.'

I drank. It was tart and had fresh mint leaves in the ice. Lots of rum. I downed the glass out of thirst and instantly felt light-headed. I started unpacking.

'Don't bother unpacking the camera. I'll talk all day but no filming. Lo siento.'

I stopped, sat back. I could hear two women speaking in the apartment next door. They laughed every so often, the type of laughter that accompanies dirty jokes.

'You were thirsty, pour yourself another.' She came back into the room with a wide bowl of beans and rice in one hand and a plate of sliced chicken and crusty bread in another. 'Sorry about no filming. I know that's what you want but it's just not … just no.'

'That's fine. I am using a lot of audio and text in the film. More and more, it seems. You know how sometimes a piece will get away from you – well, this one is way away from me.'

'Film is a fine place to start, but when you're trying to get to the truth of Henry Black … let it get away from you, I think.'

I marvelled at hearing her say his name. Henry Black. The name took on whole new meanings. And Luisa had a way of looking right at me that was exhilarating. It may have been a cultural difference, but it was such a change from Dee's intense aloofness. I felt like Luisa would crawl into my mouth as I spoke.

'You and Henry were lovers, no?'

'No, I never met him, Luisa. I know that seems odd for someone who is supposed to capture the man on film, but I feel like I know him now. Except for when he was in Mexico.'

'Well, there is no secret flip side to him. He was Henry in Toronto and Henry in Salina Cruz. Except maybe the mushrooms. He came for them almost as much as he came to see me. Hallucinogenics, they let his writing hand run "true" – whatever that means. Personally, I can live without them. They're like trashy novels. There is too much work to do. And I don't need that kind of self-gratification.'

'How come you don't stay in the villa up on the hill?'

'A few reasons. That was where Henry and I lived and he filled it with his smell, his stuff. It was never really my place. And I missed being around people, I am a people gal.' She turned to the wall. 'Andriena! No sirve para nada!' Howls of assent and laughter shook back through the wall. Luisa shrugged, 'Andriena likes to talk about her husband's dangling thing. I need that laughter around me.' She turned serious. 'Henry was looking for something. He was a very brave man. Brave and foolish. Stupidly foolish, not endearing foolish. He sought a magic that was not his to discover. My country was a cryptic theology that he wanted to ... how do you say, invoke? so it would intervene, you know, divinely, and save him. It would not. I would not. The blood will not be redeemed. Or forgotten.' She paused, gauging my response.

'He sacrificed everything for art: love, life, human compassion. He is not to be forgiven. Pitied and feared perhaps, but not forgiven.' She smiled again. 'Do not be sad. The world is a beautiful place. Let us go out for a cocktail and then I will walk you back to the villa. He has a few poems hidden away that I will pull out for you.'

♦

To the Rio Coatzacoalcos

skull a fajo that
reluctant maguey worm tangled in
tensions a will, a will without

solace and ranging a plumed serpent over
the cracked hands of each morning
paling, sluicing into other hands

this is not a complaint;
an affluent diatribe at worst,
an inflammatory gesture at the behest
of just one last conjugal wish
that teeters on the soft brink of an
unalphabetized oblivion, a leap
out of faith, into
a latent green hit, feathery ribs, cap
rooted in beauty, shit

a zephyr but further, further

(looking back, I wouldn't
have it say so much)

off the scale tipped
by an unseen thumb, riverbanks
pulling the poem along and needed
only this, this small act

silenced out there
is there a
is there

♦

Reign

Quickly the ground rules were set. I found myself one
day in the company of the royal couple in the west
porch dining area. It was late morning and Peter was
eating pastries while complaining about the mice
keeping him awake. Ekaterina was not listening.
Instead she was staring out at the horses by the stable.
They were rolling in the dirt by the creek bank,
making wet happy noises and thumping their hooves
against the ground. When she was not staring out at
their antics, she was staring at me. I watched her
watch me in the reflections in the silver. She was rest-
less and shuffled her skirts with the sound of inconsis-
tent rain. Sparrows darted onto the table and I
motioned them away, moving closer to where she sat.
On her plate sat a pastry with one large bite taken out
of it. It didn't look like she was going to finish it.

I had been trained a soldier, an elite soldier
destined to be a leader of men, and here I was staring
at pastries. I was more than that – a bodyguard, a
messenger, an advisor – but at that moment all I was
doing was staring at pastries. You must realize that
I didn't care. I was fed. I was around this beautiful
woman. Sure, I'd be a leader, a captain, a count, but
then, there, in 1756, I was just living. I also had a job to
do – Ekaterina had to learn Russian ways, Russian
politics, what it would take to win over the Russian

people. You see, already we were planning to place our princess on the throne and get rid of that pesky pretender.

'Peter, could you fetch me my glasses by the bed?' She spoke this while staring at the horses.

'Why don't you send him?' I hated the way he said 'him.'

'Oh, Peter, I don't want him seeing all my rumpled bedclothes. You go.'

He sighed. A blob of custard had fallen on his pants near the crotch. The Grand Duke laboured to his feet and shuffled off into the palace. He was not king yet, and, if I had my way, he would never be. My lot was with her; she told me she was going to rule Russia one day.

Once he had left, Ekaterina immediately got up and walked over to me. I kept my gaze low so that I ended up looking at the front of her dress. She came close, within inches of my shoulder. Her breath had green cut grass and sleep in it. She stayed there, close, shifting slightly from one foot to the other. I can only guess she was examining my face, my hair. I was not scared and, in fact, was delighted at her bold move. She moved away, but not until after brushing her hand across my neck and making a low *mmmmm* sound.

♦

Luisa took out her bicycle and I walked beside her wobbly path until we reached the bottom of the hill on which the villa perched. During the climb, Luisa muttered, 'As if one were to talk to a man's house, knowing not what gods or heroes are.' She may have been quoting a poem – it sounded familiar. It was surrounded by flowers and breeze. Bees droned and bumped around the three rooms. One found itself caught in an old phonograph and its complaint projected out and echoed through the near-empty rooms.

Luisa dug out a stack of papers from several cabinets and handed them over without preface. A stack of poems almost a forearm thick. We stood on the patio, several arm lengths apart, and looked out over the ocean.

Luisa turned and came towards me. She came close, reached up and touched my neck. Closer yet, she leaned in and kissed me on the lips. A few seconds, her lips salty and cool. She pulled back a few centimetres, looked me in the eyes, said, 'For Henry.'

◆

Last night I dreamed of maggots, of putrefaction, of flesh boiling with decay. I dreamed of annihilation, of the absolute beauty of complete and utter dispersal.

Last night I dreamed of a bird, a heron or crane, pegged to a tree and stinking of rot. I dreamed that this bird was not a crucified thing hanging there unrepentant, that this corpse was not a sign, not a harbinger, not forsaken at all. I dreamed that revulsion came home, squirmed free, dropped and rested in my palm, twelve wriggling white angels perched on the edge of what could be. I dreamed I stared hard at the dead body, his arms crossed over his torso, his feet pointed outward, his eyes wide, his penis sunken. I dreamed that I began speaking and the body floated up, leaving a plain wet sheet and as I spoke louder and louder it floated higher and higher. My voice roared and boomed as it rose up until it was a tiny dot hung at the end of my words.

In the morning, when I rose, I wrote the word 'shroud' on the notepad next to my bed. I had to think more about it.

It was the only sleeping dream I had the whole time I was in Oaxaca.

♦

SLOW FADE-IN
Jay is reading in a high-backed wicker chair on the small patio overlooking the sea. The stucco sea, a stucco wall, and a single clay pot are behind him. After a few moments, he begins reading from a thin book. He does not look up.

> *A careless proposition as if*
> *it didn't mean as much as*
> *it did — a faint but desperate*
> *clutching at love, those moments*
> *that make up the love narrative*
>
> *they may not be assembled*
> *ordered, those fragments those*
> *late morning fucks remain*
> *unwoven, uncollected*

my love, my passion, those
lives I live resenting
my own narrative frame

such tensions are bound to
a strange dispersal and
pitiful concessions

presences, presences
they undermine all we are

Jay stops reading, closes the book. He looks down at the ground off-camera. LONG SLOW FADE.

♦

I felt like I was cheating on Dee. With Luisa, with Oaxaca, with mushrooms. I was abdicating responsibility, jumping ship. But I had no choice. To do the film, to give that to Dee, I had to find another way, escape the story so I could return absolutely storyless.

Luisa left me alone at the villa and I spent most of the time reading, rereading, the sea a new context for Henry's cramped lines, the thin, tenuous softcover books so much flotsam.

Luisa was out of reach. Her relationship with Henry would remain an untapped resource. I could not bring myself to pillage it. But she did lead me back to the writing and Henry's books. Luisa would roll the words, the lines around in her mouth like ice cubes and then spit them out like sunflower seed husks. Luisa's joy and exuberance surprised me after Dee's disdain.

I missed Dee. I would return to her. But I vowed to return empty-handed.

♦

In the footsteps of Charles Olson, Henry asked and asked about the mushrooms, his poor Spanish all over the province. Wherever I mentioned Henry's name, the bartender or the farmer or the taxi driver nodded and said, 'Si, él buscamos para hongo, para seta.' They all shook their heads sadly, as if they respectfully pitied the man they referred to. I madly riffled through my Spanish-English dictionary and asked where he went to find the mushrooms. They all just shook their heads sadly. A woman in Pochutla grabbed my shirt and stared into my eyes: 'No digas otra palabra.' Then walked away without looking back. I ripped out my dictionary: not a word, not another word, not even a word. Was she saying there was no trace of the mushrooms or was it a command, a warning? The latter seemed more likely given her facial expression.

I was close.

I tried the mushrooms that people gave me when I inquired into them. I had tried some in Toronto a few years back and liked the gentle but deep hallucinations. It felt like being in a Dali painting back then and still did here, but maybe a little more intensely. My landscape undulated as the dusty bus floated and spun through collapsing valleys and sparkling whirlpools. I am not a regular drug user. It took years before I would even sample – my prairie-boy prudishness averting my hand at parties, making me decline politely. The first ones I bought in Salina Cruz were from an American named Chid. 'Psilocybe mexicanaaaaa, my man – the elixir of life! Here, these are from Huautla de Jimenez. Top grade. Not the strongest but no dung for these sweet babies. Forty bucks American'll get you at least a week of heaven.' He had a Hawaii-bright print t-shirt and a bandana.

Charles Olson was here, too: a shelf of American poetry in Tehuantepec, a signature on a barroom wall, a photograph in a gallery in a small town I never did find out the name of.

I followed the mushrooms as they became more and more intense up the valley towards Veracruz on the other coast. In the valley I found that the small towns often had *velada* ceremonies after sunset. I was out of honey and nutmeg so was eating the mushrooms straight now. Up here, they were always fresh, picked that day. The mushrooms gathered me in to the landscape, planted visions in the red soil, invoked a sun that called out all my previous illusions. I was grandiose, standing there on a deserted road, mumbling proclamations at the wind. I was a prophet, a poet, a general, a king. A prairie boy waited for me to return to Canada.

♦

Higher yet – the altitude alone made me dizzy. My nose bled constantly. I thought of returning to Luisa but that would seem like an avoidance, a submission to the power of the obvious.

Dreamworlds folded into dreamworlds, but the last seemed to be the luminous city of Tuxtepec. There, the farmers and herders moved in a kind of trance. They embraced everyone they met and had open, wise faces. The local Mazatec ate the mushrooms only at night in absolute darkness, drawing almost the entire community to the fire. Families ate the mushrooms together: father, mother, children, uncles and aunts all seated around a bonfire gazing into the future. 'If you eat them in the daylight you will go mad,' they said. 'The dead of night is most conducive to visions into the obscurities, the mysteries, the perplexities of existence.' The leader, a stocky shaman with a voice that seemed to come from a deep underground lake, held me in his arms and whispered that I should share with him these revelations.

A Frenchman stood out in his khaki and spectacles. He sat near me the first night and began to lecture in an authoritative voice. He spoke of 'transcendental subjectivity' and quoted Husserl's word 'intersubjectivity.' He leaned forward in awe. 'They sit together glowing with an inner light, they dream and realize, suddenly with a flash of their eyes in the firelight, and converse with each other, presences seated there together, their bodies immaterial, voices from outside their communality. The *velada* is a therapeutic catharsis. The chemicals of revelation open the circuits of thought and vision and communication. Mind-manifesting. Modalities of the spirit freed.' He was clearly mad. Books tumbled out of his knapsack.

The second night in Tuxtepec he introduced himself as Azee and said he was looking for a woman he had lost in the wilderness, a woman he was both in love with and studying. He was a twitchy man, verbose but absolutely ill at ease in the world. He told me about what he learned from the ceremonies the last four months he'd been here, leaning over his notes:

If death is total integration, then naturally life is disintegration, and when seeking love, when seeking to become whole, we put one toe in our own deaths ... so, if love is a little like death (a little death), death is pure love, the great cosmic orgasm.

He stopped and looked up as if surprised I was still listening. 'Oh, my dear man, you must experience the *temazcal* up on the mountain, I will take you there. Maria will take you.' He read on:

Every event, every being can suddenly turn itself into its own symbol and lose in action what it gains in permanence.

The Mazatecs say that the mushrooms speak. If you ask a shaman where his imagery comes from, he is likely to reply, 'I didn't say it, the mushrooms did.' 'It is not I who speak,' said Heraclitus, 'it is the logos.'

Intoxicated by the mushrooms, the fluency, the ease, the aptness of expression, what I became capable of astounded me. At times it was as if I were being told what to say. The spontaneity the mushrooms liberated was perceptual, linguistic. I felt like I was the receptacle of a fervent, lucid discourse. Outside me.

Cross-legged on the floor in the dark, close to the fire, inhaling the hot incense of copal, the shaman sat with a furrowed brow and the marked mouth of speech. He invoked Quetzalcóatl and at the end of each phrase he said *tzo* – 'says' – like a rhythmic punctuation. Says, says, says. It is said.

I returned to my bed and sat near the weak firelight, smoke stinging my eyes. I paged through Dee's novel, looking for something. I could hardly read the print.

Reign

Our bodies became incremental around each other. First a hip. Then a thigh, then a buttock. It would be easy to say she handled me like a piece of meat and that may be close to the truth, but at the time, each touch felt like a romantic interlude, like a rendezvous by moonlight.

And the first time I touched her was by moonlight. The Regent's quarters, where I was staying at this time, not yet assuming the role of Grand Master, were directly across from the royal quarters with the kitchen and dining room in between. One glorious night I went into the kitchen to cook an egg on the one wood stove Evegeny keeps going all night. I took two eggs and broke them over a skillet. I had no light except the moon which shone through a squat window near the ceiling. I knelt down to put a few more chunks of wood into the stove and while I was there on all fours, she appeared.

Now, I had been thinking a lot about what this moment might mean and the dangers for my career and life it would bring. At any moment, if I didn't please her entirely she could raise the alarm, state simply and plainly that I had assaulted her, and I would be quickly dispatched. The royal couple were not intimate, I had heard – she couldn't stand his childish pranks and his sickly state. But they were betrothed and Elizabeth would not abide any embar-rassing displays that might weaken her son's claim to the crown. I was going to be instrumental in placing Ekaterina in power but even now, she had free reign. It was that clear; I had no power.

I was still in my nightshirt and a cold draft swooped up it. I wasn't that worried about my undignified position if I remember right.

We regarded each other briefly before I turned my gaze down. I heard her approach and then I felt her climb on top of my back. I stayed there, facing the still-open fire and a blue-painted earthenware jar that held ashes. She was not heavy and straddled me with ease. All I could see of her was her feet, bare with her slip-pers kicked off to the side. They were perfect: well-kept but not coddled, shapely but strong. I could not tell if she was wearing undergarments beneath her nightclothes. Slowly she reached back, her weight shifting above me, to pull up my nightshirt and reveal my ass. She stroked it briefly, gave it a light slap.

It was then that I dared. I felt the need to recipro-cate in some way. I shifted my weight to one hand and reached to touch the top of her left foot. The eggs crackled and spat above us. The white moon laughed.

She got off abruptly a few minutes later. That was enough. She went to a cupboard and took out a clay jar from behind a stack of plates on the top shelf and handed it to me as she left. I recognized the jar as one sealed by master chef Andropov. Her legend was just beginning to spread across Europe – her magic fish dishes, her sweets, her absolutely original creations. It was said the Pugachov Rebellion was caused by her glazed pheasant with pineapple.

The wax lifted with a twist of my fingernail. A miracle, a taste on my finger: pear – strong mountain pear from near Kursk or Kharkov, picked by olive hands and shipped in ice barges up the Dnepr and overland between crates of frozen lamb – and mint, fresh fragrant mint from the Riga lowlands, slightly crushed when only two days old. Grape juice mollified the two flavours, wound them about each other and demanded another flick of the tongue. These flavours, even today, cause my body to stiffen, my passions to turn.

Her choreography of me continued. Her desire became animated into my daily routine, my official duties, the way I positioned myself near her at court. She was insistent but not a tyrant – she carefully weighed any discomfort to me, any ways in which I might be injured. And it did become physical enough that my safety was an issue.

Late one night she found me and beckoned me into the ballroom in the south wing. The lights had been extinguished and there was no moon, so the only light came in from the clouded sky and indirectly from other windows in the palace. We ascended the wide staircase normally used by elegantly arrayed dignitaries and social debutantes during the St Peter's Day and harvest celebrations. We walked across the ballroom floor, lost in the huge gloom of the expansive room. I knew, by memory, that huge murals ran along the top of the lengthwise walls. Invisible czars and heroes roamed the dark expanses above the ghostly windows.

She was somewhere behind me, her soft-shoed feet making no sound. Mine thudded and echoed, making me wonder if she had snuck off to leave me for dead in this strange dim pandemonium. When we reached the opposite end of the floor, faced with an identical dim rise of stairs, she touched my arm to stop. I started, not knowing if she was real or phantom. She bade me to disrobe with a small twirling motion of her index finger while staring at my waist. She rarely spoke and depended on hand gestures and her direct demanding gaze to arrange my presence. On this night, I was to drape myself over the bronze statue of Charles. I awkwardly mounted the regal bronze, clutching the cold metal chest, wincing at the sting against my thighs and hands. I must have looked slightly pitiful next to the enlarged and regally posed and clothed physique of Charles I. Perched there, I heard her breathing escalate as she reached beneath her nightclothes and brought herself to orgasm. It did not take long and, still breathing heavily, she waved me down. She kissed my shoulder and turned away. Several paces away, so that she was invisible in the dark, she turned and said, 'You may now call me "Figchen" ... I would like that. And you should know that I have a profound aversion to straight lines.'

This was two weeks before we began planning to oust Peter.

I have killed men before but rarely one who was pleading for his life. And, in truth, I was not the one who, almost gently, squeezed the life from the thin man attempting to buy us off.

As Ekaterina rode into St Petersburg to maintain her claim to the throne, my brother Alexei and I were charged with making sure Peter was not chartered away to rebuild an attempt to reclaim his place. Surely there were some Russians who wanted him in power; they would dearly love to have him safe in their hands so they could use his blood again. We took him from Oranienbaum in a covered carriage with three other carriages of the same type leaving before and after. He was to be placed under house arrest at a small estate in Schlusselburg inland away from the lake. One hundred and fifty hand-picked soldiers resided at the estate and another entire battalion was within an hour of the location. It was critical that Peter stay put.

Alexei knew this better than me and he was nervously pacing when Peter was brought to us. Peter had demanded the opportunity to pledge allegiance to Ekaterina and concede the throne. When he was carried in, though, these well-intentioned sentiments fell by the wayside and he began drunkenly shouting insults at us and his wife.

'That bitch! You have been duped by a bitch of monumental proportions. She can't rule; she's a country girl, a common whore, a plaything. She just wants to run around and sleep with men – you know, have sex with them. It's all she thinks about! She doesn't know about drills and protocol and the important stuff. She lies. Why would strong military men like you be fooled by her? She's just a … '

Alexei had moved closer and knocked him over with a soft backhand across his head. Peter fell over crying and screeching at us that we were insane, the word a wet, slurred sob.

I said, hoping to quiet him, 'Ekaterina will make a fine monarch for Russia. She loves Russia. You despise it. How can you rule a country you despise? Tell me that. You, with your Prussian arrogance, your incessant belittling of everything my family holds dear. The Fatherland will not abide – and so, we have a mother to guide Russia.'

'Your mother is a godforsaken … ' he sputtered, not finding the word in Russian he was looking for.

'Gift,' I replied for him. He screeched even louder, a piercing keen that made us wince.

He slowed and, collecting himself slightly, asked where Elizaveta was. The Vorontsova socialite had been his unofficial consort for many months now. She had been taken to the compound but kept in separate quarters. She complained ferociously about the state of her rooms and demanded to be served meals at the proper times. I empathized with his desire to be near his lover – my thoughts even at that moment straying to Ekaterina, ensconced and breathless within the walls of the Summer Palace.

His voiced ascended again. 'She, she will be queen, she will rule next to me.' His lack of awareness of the situation astounded me.

Alexei looked over at me and in his look was the assertion that he was going to act for the queen and that he would take the consequences. I knew what the look meant. Ekaterina's last words before she left hung between us: 'Peter must be dealt with absolutely, finished.'

Alexei bore down on the king, put one hand over his mouth, the other on his throat, and pressed. For the sake of the country, my brother quietly executed the one person in Russia who might threaten my Ekaterina's place. I loved him for that even while I shuddered in horror as Peter's body jerked and groaned. Even as he quaked to stillness, I was both resolved and saddened. I could not meet Alexei's eyes as he stood up. I placed my hand on his shoulder, comforted his weeping as we walked from one of the last pitiful turns of empire-building.

Two nights later, Ekaterina would slap my face as we stood next to her bed. She pointed to the door. As I left, she whispered, 'It was easy, an easy out. It's what history says is the right thing to do.' She was tearing up but her voice did not waver. 'I want it done differently.' I learned then that Russia, the world and I were on the verge of reinvention. This woman, a full foot shorter than I, glaring up at me, was to be the inventor.

In a speech three days later, from the balcony of the Summer Palace, Ekaterina announced that Peter III had passed away in fever from hemorrhoidal colic. Even then, she had a flair for brilliantly ironic propaganda – the kind that made the country believe in nothing but her.

It was July 1, 1762, and my figchen was sitting astride all of Russia.

It had something to do with language, a gorgeous miscommunication which resolved itself into a bed bedecked with a queen, a man and a horse much embarrassed at its predicament.

I was ecstatic – an excitement undampened by the prospect of playing second fiddle to a quarter horse named Kovlik, undeterred by the elaborate winches and pulleys required to hoist the beast above the bed, and only slightly intimidated by the large black-purple penis that hung in the air like an amputated heart.

I was at home around horses. My father had a dozen well-bred horses on his compound at all times and took pride in helping his trainers exercise and appoint them on afternoons he didn't have pressing business. I learned to ride early, around six or seven years, I think, and had rubbed elbows with some of the top breeders in the region. Kovlik was a good horse.

I picked him because of his docile nature. He was of a line long reserved for stylish ladies and royal daughters. I, like him, knew the pleasures of ease and letting the reins guide you where they will.

It had something to do with language, with dialect; I had no idea the word could fall between us so ungainly, so immense. The measure of her words was so precise as we moved through the daily rituals and courtesies of the palace, that I tended to put pressure on every syllable, every nuance of inflection, every pause, every sound, guttural, whispered, sighed, that emanated from her. I took her word and loved it as a gift.

This word threw me; but gifts are not to be questioned and I did not. The word was 'loshad,' elegant in its simplicity, muscular, its pivot the strong liquid 'l' which, in certain dialects, dove into an even deeper loquacious 'w' sound. The word eluded its meaning and, in doing so, precipitated the scene of misdirected desires I shall now relate.

The winches and pulleys I had brought in from the shipyards, along with a fitted tarp cradle made especially to load and unload livestock on the wharf. Instead of a tall crane I had to instruct the local machinist to bolt the improvised joists to the roof of the bedroom and sent the lead pulley out the window and below where I would have a team of horses ready to hoist on command. The horse was in place and pacified with a generous bucket of barley – which I second-guessed, worrying about gas at inopportune moments, but then shrugged off as uncontrollable. The horse made a mockery of the bedroom's finery and seemed monstrous in such a context. Its strangeness was exhilarating in a certain way as well – like a snake in a washing bowl or a bird in the kitchen. Kovlik seemed amused by the whole process and played the clown by chewing on linen, flapping his lips and chortling at our protests.

You see, dear reader, 'loshad' means both 'horse' and 'large burly man,' depending on which side of the Baltic you are speaking on. A slight inflection, a longer liquid rolling off the tongue, and there we were, suspended on the edge of absurdity, suspended on the edge of history, suspended in the throes of language.

◆

On my way down another unmapped road, the sun curling feline around my feet, I looked up to see Henry slouched under a Joshua tree. This was our second meeting in Oaxaca. His head was bowed and he was drooped over one knee as if asleep. I ran forward, low to the ground like I was avoiding enemy gunfire, and threw myself next to him. My arms enfolded his decrepit body and we stayed like that through three ascensions of the predatory sun. I stayed with Henry in his hour of need. I dared not lift his face, he needed to conserve his strength. There, there, Henry. There, there. I would be going home soon.

♦

Azee left for Argentina – but before he left he brought me to the house of a medicine woman named Maria Sabinez. Azee nervously kissed my lips as he fled back down the path. I chewed the rich black beans and bread Maria set in front of me. She did not say a word but bade me empty my pockets into a small box that she then stowed away in another room. I was here for the *temazcal* sweat – it wouldn't happen until dusk. We waited. It seemed part of the process.

The sweat was held high in the hills and I gasped for oxygen as we ascended. The mountains glowed blue and teal and small rocks echoed as they clattered down the path behind us. Maria had held my hand as we departed but now walked ahead as a line of ten people walked single file up the mountainside.

I was prepared like meat, my body lathered and shoved into a holy oven. The skin-ensconced womb smelled like blood: sharp, wet, salty, as if the ocean had swelled to pick up the tiny pod and carry it away. An old woman bathed me and tossed my clothes aside. With metal tongs she carried hot boulders and heaved them into the hut. She slathered oil on my body, rubbing vigorously all over, even abruptly and without concern between my legs, over my penis and scrotum. The heat billowed against me, blew through my mouth, skin, lungs, bones. My body felt suddenly precarious, as if in a breeze it would disintegrate entirely, easily and blissfully.

In that belly, in that horrific undulation of flesh, in that cataclysmic heat I foresaw what the end of my film must be.

◆

The first time I had seen Henry was in Xoxocotlan during the Day of the Dead celebrations. It was my fifth day in Oaxaca and I was already drifting to the northern mushroom fields. I was moving through the hallucinations smoothly by then and found myself in the midst of a city filled with flowers and tombs. Cempasuchitl flowers and memorial candles sparked and flared as I wandered through the streets, people around me laughing and wailing with the same intensity. Altars were filled with offerings of fruit, orange, red and purple flowers, and food like bread and cakes, as well more personal tokens, necklaces, mescal, cigarettes, letters and bright dolls. The dead will return to visit and enjoy the offerings made to them. Stoic but proud-looking men and women would stoop and pick up a ripe yellow mango or stop and place a trinket into their pockets. People would not look at the honoured guests but would bow their heads as they passed, 'Gracias, gracias.' The dead were among us and it was a privilege. And I was dead, too. In my wraith-like state of wonderment, I was placated, women would avert their eyes, men would mutter their thanks as I passed. I ate, I feasted on the living adoration they bestowed on me. Flowers decked my head and shoulders. It was a rite of passage. It was a theatre of the spirit.

It was then that I saw Henry across the market square. He was sitting near a fountain with garlands around one arm. He was watching me as I moved through the limbs and torsos and heads that butted and encircled my less substantial frame. The crowd held. Henry vanished. The sun set and the Day of the Dead was over.

Seeing him, I knew I was right to come to Mexico. This was my path.

♦

I stayed there in the hills with the Mazatec for two weeks. An old woman let me stay in a clay outbuilding with two goats. A fire pit and straw mattress greeted me each morning as I returned roundabout from the *velada*. The bright green anoles sang verdant songs of love in three-part harmony as I teetered into sleep. *Reign* sat next to my bed, read and reread. Dee, too, visited me then. She came through the door and scolded me for my romanticism and my lazy lapse into the mystical. I just laughed and chased her out, snakes coiled around each of my wrists. This was my trip. Henry was my project. He needed me more. For the first time I felt pity for the man. I felt pity for Henry, and felt piteous in my own right. Tuxtepec had instilled pity in me and I was ready to return to the living.

♦

Dee picked me up at the airport outside Halifax. We were quiet in the car (she drove even though it was my rented car) and it seemed as if she was afraid of what I was going to report. It may have been about Luisa or maybe she knew of Henry's drug obsession. It suited me fine, though – I hated trying to capture a trip or articulate an extended series of events. I guess I am not a storyteller.

She saw something in my eyes, though, and she pursed her lips in anger. How quickly she had come to know me, admonish me, fear for my safety. But she was not my mother, and she did not let herself become entangled. I could slip off into never-never land, for all she cared. Maybe the prairie boy was back, maybe he wasn't. Regardless, I was ready to finish my film. I was going to throw out most of what I had done. One step back.

We careened down the highway at break-neck speed.

♦

I set up the camera in the kitchen near the door and asked Dee to re-enact the day I first came to the farmhouse. I stood her next to the sink facing away from me. Then I had to run out to the shed to get the fat cat. I grabbed a fistful of beets from the cold room and rubbed dirt all over them. I reached up and smudged Dee's cheek with a dab of mud.

She watched my eyes for signs of madness. She had been distant, furious with me for my unspoken transgressions in Mexico. We had skirted each other for days. I could see she was still pissed off, but, oddly, agreed to play along with me.

I got behind the camera and asked her to tell me that she would never speak of Henry. She did and turned around finally, like that first day, but stopped and frowned. 'Should I be speaking to you or to the camera pretending it's you?'

'It doesn't matter. The words and the light are the only important things.' The camera consistently made her nervous and I just wanted her to forget about it.

'So, you freely admit that art is a mockery of the real, that it is just a sham, a hasty re-creation. Don't you think that somehow, haphazardly repeating that first day on film is disrespectful? No stupid film will capture its essence, capture the romance, er, the tension, the magic, whatever … '

'So, what, you think writing is some pristine realism, that perfect container, a conduit to some truth, is that what you believe? Am I too inauthentic for you? A sham?'

We were shouting, surprised by our own vehemence. We realized we were arguing the other's position: she was the anti-realist and I was the documentary man. Despite the absurdity of our stands we glared at each other – me, with the camera still tucked into my shoulder like a weapon.

'Wait, wait … ' the realization came with a flood of understanding, 'this is a narrative time issue.' She looked at me without comprehension, but then softened and nodded.

♦

How about this. Death is a theory of art. A theory that proposes that the imprint of a human life is magic, immortal. At the moment we die, we arrive at a final conception of residual effects, what the residue means. Yes, 'means' – I am sure it is here, elusive, taciturn, mischievous.

Dee's house now was a magic place, a place where time slowed and the rhythms of the earth thrummed up through the floorboards. In the mornings I pressed my hand against the wall by my bed and felt the sun pressing back. Roots laced in through the stones in the cellar, twined up into the joists. Pollen fell under a sleeping tongue.

I had noticed in pictures that Henry had one finger missing. His right ring finger was gone, missing right up to the knuckle. It was easy to miss – it is an odd finger to be missing, in the middle, not an index or pinky. When I asked people about it – his sister, publisher, landlord – they all came up with different stories. Lost in a printing press. Cut off by a car engine fan trying to save a cat who had been sleeping on the warm block. He was caught stealing in Yemen, imprisoned in a steel box, had it cut off in a formal ceremony with a machete.

When I told Dee the stories she laughed. 'Henry is just a collection of stories. That's all he is, you know that.'

'Well, no, he was a real man, too. Wasn't he?'

'How do you know? Did you ever meet him?'

'No. But you have. You've slept with him, for heaven's sake. You can't say he wasn't real.'

'Oh, yes, I can. I have a story about us "sleeping together" but that's all.' She said 'sleeping together' in a gossipy lisp. She leaned towards me. We were back on the couch smoking. It was by now a comfortable habit, a habit that grew out of suspicion, worked its way through intrigue, and crested into sheer comfort and languid indulgence. I thought she might be leaning to kiss me, and was preparing to be suitably confused, but instead she pulled out a folded sheet of paper and handed it to me.

It was a poem.

'Henry left it in a folder of financial stuff where I would find it.'

It was typed in the familiar faded typewriter print that I recognized as Henry's early writing:

> *The Last One*
>
> *lucidly, I misread*
> *the last thing unsaid in the vast*
> *commingled syntax of two and knowledge.*

> *acknowledged, this is what I tell myself,*
> *a kind of mantra but decentring instead:*

> *my words stand, I*
> *echo, the remainder.*

Period.

I opened the book again. It was his most popular, if poetry could ever be called 'popular.' The title was *Pandemonium* and the cover was a psychedelic watercolour with concentric circles of purple, red and blue. It was dedicated to Ishtar.

    The book is divided into three sections: father, son, spirit. He seemed to be exploring ideas of divinity but without much reference to the Bible. I flipped through the book and plucked out lines at random:

> *in trusting the rush of penance in the thighs*
> *they buried their dead in a sitting posture*
> *as the red-faced prick thundered on*
> *holding, holding, the last piece of bread*
> *sexing just enough of the liturgy to know*
> *in justifying all that is not yet to be*
> *the holy water was frozen*
> *cataloguing makes exceptions, resists ending*
> *an ancient, poised continuum*

Who's there?

The door half-open. I peer out, knowing I will see nothing but an empty hallway, knowing it was Henry's ghost.

It is a tender haunting which disturbs my work – a light tap on my door or thin window. If my room were a skull it would be a caress on my brow, a chuck under my chin. It is a knowledge that haunts the movement of air in Dee's house, that creases the flow of time over an evening so I look up with a start, ideas fleeing.

Who's there?

It is an inane question, a question that scouts the topography of the dark room, constructs the shadows into the known, moulds the ordered choreography of furniture into arms, legs, sculpts dawn from the horizon. Outside my door there is a 'who' who may be there to answer. 'Who' is Henry. I open my door again, walk down the hallway, down stairs, peer out into the mist and leaves. Everything is wet or recently wet. The high clouds dimly reflect the last of sun but the sky behind is dark, already showing stars.

Who's there?

Just out of sight, Henry ducks my gaze, grinning, knowing I know it is him but not deigning to give me confirmation. Nothing so solid, nothing so sure. All our arts fail, he says in his absolute absence.

Who's there?

Anyone. It is a quest, a question reaching for anyone. Searching for contact beyond the abyss of our skins – yes, yes, respond, say you are not dead, Henry, say you are still breathing, cursing, being a bastard, writing, say you are still writing those lines I read and reread.

Who's there?

I will ask this question until I die.

One day, some day, I will know how to let this ghost in.

♦

There is a story about Henry becoming unruly at a conference at the University of Toronto. The story goes that Henry, both hungover and reinebriated, threatens to kick James Healey in the head if he doesn't shut up. One version has it that Henry has to be restrained and several aging professors have to grapple with him to keep him from going onstage to confront Healey. Another has the shouting match escalate to a crescendo where Henry lobs a gob of spit towards Healey. Still a third has Henry passing out mid-insult and being carted out over a bulky grad student's shoulder.

He had given a paper earlier in the day: an effusive, rambling reflection on the poetry of a dead friend. In it he speaks to his friend like he is there, calling him an angel or an aura or just by name. He speaks softly into the microphone about their time together and I imagine him whispering anecdotes, poems, hyperboles, becoming quieter as he draws each segment to a close so the last word is inaudible. It is something about presence, something about love.

He sits still (his sacroiliac bad at this point) through his talk, only his hand moving over his face, brow, skull, the nape of his neck at intervals. He looks tired, bored with the whole ordeal. Life for him has become a stagy conference filled with people who think they know the answer.

The paper he gives is published in a Guelph literary supplement. He has dispensed with paragraph breaks and begins it with a quote from *The Epic of Gilgamesh* – not one you'd expect, nothing about mourning, but one about forgetting, the libation of forgetting.

Is this desperation I sense in his writing hand, his signature effluence gone shaky, barely cogent?

These traces, they are hot coals under my bare feet. This disinterment, an uneasy ingression.

♦

Henry is constructing the film and the film is constructing me. I am a product of formal concerns; the process of disclosure un-invents what previously I had held as all-encompassing, sure, at my disposal. In a single deft turn of phrase (Henry's poem, Dee's prose contraptions) my power to discern me from them, life from death, transparency from a latticework of ingrained behaviours – well, they collapse, they shatter. Yes, I am the dreamy sort, the kind who travels thousands of kilometres to confirm a hunch about love, the kind who believes there is room in the world for absolute grace, the kind who would devastate three books on perennials trying to find the history of the trumpet flower, the kind who will embrace the completely dead to the point of nearly dying myself. Yes, yes, I am compelled to shatter. Aren't we all? Unless we are fools or prone to violence, aren't we all prone to shattering?

Yes, I have been thinking this. The question arises. You know it. The question: should I, dare I, kill myself at the end of the film? It is a question. It begs itself – a complete system in and of itself, complete with the most ingenious escape hatch of all. Complete. The character recedes from the set into that wondrously artful fade-out. Is this not art? It is a matter of closure, of semiotic integrity, of narrative power. Complete closure. The end.

♦

Reign

It was well known that a famous French philosopher was courting Ekaterina with letters. When I came to her late at night she would often be bent over her desk writing letters with books opened and scattered around her, on the bed, at her feet. Voltaire, I think, was his name and the well-read people at court fawned over his books, dropped his writing into conversations to assert how European they were becoming. I am not a man of letters or philosophy. Matters of state and my own passions serve to ground my world enough that the lofty prattle I hear only makes me think what sad deprived lives these people live. You live life, you don't pore over it in books.

Obviously, Ekaterina was one who moved between both. She seemed to genuinely enjoy his writing and quite often read parts to me aloud. At other times, though, it was clear she was toying with him – chortling at his romantic overtures, mocking his easily perked ego. At the bottom of his page he signed 'The hermit of Ferney.' That was all I could make out over her shoulder. I did not know French like she did so she stumbled over the text, quickly trying to translate it into Russian. Almost inevitably she apologized after reading aloud, saying it lost its edge or power in the translation. She lived in other languages while I stayed at home in Russian. My figchen – I missed her when she was caught up in her reading or in her endless letters and writings. But Ekaterina taught me early on that tolerance and loyalty are what she stands for. And I loved that in her and, so, stood for those things, too. I am not naturally self-effacing – my blood is built on the backs of dominant men. I am, first of all, a military man, a man of battle, sweat, decent but certainly indelicate. Ekaterina, she taught me that the sweet scents come not from crushing the leaf but from knowing what time of day to stoop close to it.

She told me she might take other lovers. Even as Grand Master of the Ordnance, my country is mine only because she chooses to have me. I stand grateful.

When Diderot came to visit she told me she might fuck him if he was not too frail. I acquiesced. This was what it meant to be an Empress's lover. Sometimes she was girlish in her coyness: 'Just a mind fuck, love, don't be mad.' And I wasn't – Diderot, after all; how could I win that battle? I feigned jealousy when she wanted me to. I am sure she knew I was faking it.

And I shared her joy when I overheard her scold the poor old bastard, 'Oh, you men of intellect, how you impute to reality what is only in your imagination!' Her high, resonant laugh crumbled the grandiose artifice of letters, the haughty self-absorbed crust of modern philosophy.

◆

Dee hunches over *Reign*, holds volumes of philosophy as she eats breakfast, pores over correspondence, tries to climb into texts to find Henry. I ask her, why her, why Catherine II? She says it is something to do with both her absolute integrity and her ability, despite that, to have her husband killed. I read closely, looking for signs of her mourning, looking for the imprint of Henry. If it is there, it is indelible.

I wander down by the creek, watch as cranes dip down to pluck frogs from the pond's bank, let apple blossoms get caught in my hair, just to prevent Henry from finding me. We are both embattled and haunted – sometimes these things being one in the same. We eat standing up, hunted, haggard. We forget to take baths, scare each other when we have forgotten the other was in the house.

Reign is as thick as my torso. My film is nearly finished, a bad trip. A thick, tense vibration fills the air. Something is going to break.

◆

Reign

Outside St Petersburg, just south of the Neva near Pella, was a stretch of marshland that we visited often. We hunted with three or four other huntsman and a small pack of dogs. Ekaterina sat high in the saddle on her horse Brilliant as we set out well before dawn. She rode astride – something that the court continued to titter about. As if a woman spreading her legs were a scandalous indiscretion rather than a matter of choice, comfort, pleasure.

I have to admit, my interest in hunting was exaggerated so that she would take me with her on these excursions. She had developed a habit of going off for full days with huntsmen from the Summer Palace, heading out south from the gardens into the hills that ran to the west along the coast towards Clesme. The huntsmen were a rangy lot, burly, unkempt, surly almost – things she would have been attracted to. You probably understand my dilemma. I was not the jealous sort but neither was I stupid. I put myself in positions where she would notice me, I caught her out of the corner of my eye and straightened my back, curled my thick arms, flashed my peacock feathers. I liked to have her look at my body. I knew that from her rooms on the south side of the palace she could see my regiment drilling, I knew that she could pick out my bulk on the field, watch my movements, notice the power I wielded at only the right moments.

My regiments loved her to the man. And they didn't take my tenuous position with her as a detriment to my command. They, too, recognized the power of this woman, recognized that I was engaged with a powerful ally in the intricate manoeuvres of love.

My queen pined away at the loss of her baby. Paul saw Ekaterina as a warm, loving aunt rather than a mother. Three years before I came to court, Paul had been born and promptly whisked off by Elizabeth. Paul was direct heir to the throne and Elizabeth did not trust (in her craggy, self-aggrandizing way) Ekaterina to keep the child. He now resided next to her quarters with Elizabeth's choice of tutors and nursemaids.

Ekaterina muttered to herself, staring across the courtyard to his windows, 'He is so small there, so frail, why can't I just hold him? Who is with him, who is watching out for the little boy, not the future monarch? It is so cold, who is holding him?'

And the father, too, was very far away. She talked about him often – Sergei Saltykov was his name. He was in Paris now, surely sleeping around the high-society scene, marketing his good looks and charm. I had never met the man but people told me that he was a slick one. Ekaterina once said he was 'handsome as the dawn.' She always spoke openly about her past lovers, knowing I was not the jealous type.

Her first lover had been a man named Zakhar, one night after they had been sledding in the park on the island. In a fishing shack they made a small fire and huddled under furs. He, too, was sent away by Elizabeth back when she held hope that Peter could work a miracle and have sex. It made me nervous, this trend of all of her lovers being sent away to far-off outposts, but I think Ekaterina chose me in part because not even Elizabeth could orchestrate a war hero's exile. Russians were too fond of war heroes to let something like that go.

The lover she spoke of most fondly was the Pole, Stanislas Poniatowski. He sounded sweet and smart from what she said of him. He had been a part of an entourage from England headed by Charles Hanbury-Williams, and she gleaned much of her knowledge of Western politics from them. Poniatowski was still around when she first noticed me and so I was able to briefly meet this one. He was bright and cheery, kind of effeminate compared to most, but I know my guardsmen are not the standard of maleness. Again, my insecurities about my lack of intellectual equality with Ekaterina surfaced but he didn't rub it in, didn't try to flourish any big words or discuss French philosophy with me. We dined on venison at the Panin estate with Ekaterina absorbed in conversation with Nikita over state affairs and Paul's health. At one point Poniatowski leaned close to me and said, 'I am still in love with her, you know.' I glanced over at her; she gave me a quick wink while still talking. He leaned a bit closer, 'But she is the boss so I concede – she has chosen you.' We sat back and smiled a forced conspiratorial smile. He leaned in again. 'Read some books. I will give you a list if you like. It makes for the best foreplay.' This last was a whisper with his rolling back in memory of pleasure. He was right. I nodded, 'Give me the list.'

I read like a drunken student, frantic and erratic. I began with Voltaire – an obvious choice. I struggled, I raged, I read some more.

I, above all, did not want to be apart from my figchen. And yet, I knew it was inevitable. Here we were, staring at each other across a dinner table, knowing we would part soon. Love stories are not what they seem. I know that now.

What play ends before the third act? What novel abandons its hero halfway, in winter quarters, on a riverbank? What novel falls in love with another medium?

♦

When schedules permitted, we dined alone in a little-used parlour in the west wing where Peter used to have his juvenile orgies and play his games. His toy soldiers still littered a large oak table in the adjacent room and the smell of old wine was soaked into the carpets. The tall windows that had been shuttered now let the orange light of the sunset flood in. These were the rooms where Peter the Great had lived and Ivan had planned his coup. Both palaces in both capitals had places like this, but St Petersburg and the Summer Palace here seemed to hold more of the future, more of the promise of what Russia could become.

'You know by now that I cannot marry you, Gregorii.'

I knew we were near the end. The unspoken had been spoken. Space, my existence, suddenly turned to stone.

♦

What valent aperture, what easy apocrypha has Henry ducked into?

Each video clip is digitized, not the romantic spools of film with the austere dark against clear filament, the rattling motors, the hot lens. But I crave that romanticism, that flagrant frame, that unapologetic contraption. Absolute versilimitude here would kill me – I need the safety of artifice, the rococo ornament catching me before I fall headlong into the viewing screen, before I join the alphabet in its archetypal march to zenith.

At Bargain Harley's in Berwick I find a used camcorder that hums at least a little, a little. Just enough to keep me awake. The one I had been using is too quiet, too easy.

The mushrooms are almost gone.

♦

JAY, as director, enters the set. He is not happy with the last take – his character is not coming across. He paces and frets for a while, rearranges the furniture, adds an overhead light, removes a microphone. His discomfort is a part of Henry.

JAY

Cut, cut, cut! The discourse we are using –
what is it? Are we thinking about a film,
about poetic language, about death, about a
dead man, about a filmmaker? Cut, cut,
cut … I need direction.

The 'I' breaks down; it is no longer stable in the face of death and language, so I enter down the long stairwell to the bedrooms. It takes several seconds for the figure to descend – slow, deliberate, as if afraid of displacing a hip or vomiting. I am tired, as if staring at a computer screen too late at night. I pass by JAY who is staring at the camera lens looking for answers. I pass by DEE who glances in my direction as if I am a ghost – intrigued, suspicious, unsure of her beliefs. My hair grows long as I walk. Longer and longer until locks threaten to trip me up. Still longer so it trails behind me. The hair is a sign of mourning, a sign of resistance, a sign of selflessness. I walk until I find a long lock of hair lying across my path on the forest floor. I set it on fire.

DEE
Stop being so foolish. Just get back to work.
Finish the script.

♦

Reign

It delights me no end to think of how much of the fate
of this country was decided by the prick and the cunt.
One's dying memoirs should be about great deeds and
state secrets but I cannot lie – my memoirs are about
the feeling of her breasts against my chest, her hand
on my cock, the way she taught me the rhythms and
sweet flourishes of her body.

They say I am unsteady now, and insist I wear these godawful underpants that itch and pinch my balls. Incontinent, they say. In what continent, I wonder. Here, in Peterhof, I stroll in the gardens, sit by the creek my father is buried next to ... but I am not here, I am not apart from my figchen. We are leaning against the railing of the Tver as it drifted up the Volga, and we had defeated the Turks and the people flocked to the shores to wave at us and throw bundles of gardenias onto the prow, and at night the boat rolled under our bed and it was then I knew you were leaving me, that you were sending me away.

That is why I went to plague-ridden Moscow – to prove my love for you. But even there, on the Volga, in 1767, I knew you were sending me away. The nobles on the boat whispered our little death, whispered speculations of marriage, lineage, heirs. The diamonds I heaped upon your bedside table gleamed like a ripe blade, contemplating the right moment to sever that thin glistening cord that tied us to the fate of Russia.

I am not apart from my figchen – she will not send me away, I will stay here in her rooms until she returns from her counsels. She will come back to me, here, and tell them that I am not unstable, I have not wet myself, I have not, I am her little king, and we will not be apart. I am not apart. I am not. I feel her in my arms now, cold, and we are shivering from the absolute clarity of each other.

◆

And this dissolution is not one. This tender finitude we face is both communal and without translation. The words turn to return us home, run us out of excuses, take us down to the beginning. Bereft of knowledge, we are allowed a plenitude and, even as our bodies starve and pale, even as we become insubstantial and piteous, the texts grow, float free.

And it is not at all inhuman, this silence, this dispersal.

The camera is running. The film is running out; I only have three tapes left.

I am worried about editing, the post-shoot arranging and rearranging. I don't want to leave Dee, leave here, I don't want to commit to finishing. I have been filming everything but anything I can use in a documentary on Henry Black. (Oh, I haven't said his last name for a while now – it seems wrong, like I am mispronouncing it.) Settling – I don't want to settle.

Something peculiar has happened between Dee and me. We hardly acknowledge the other's existence, we pass by each other and only in retrospect remember that we've passed by each other, that the other is here in the house. Yesterday I said 'Your tea water is boiling' to my bedroom window because I had passed her on the stairs and thought that she should know in case it boiled over. We interact only when she is acting out her novel, when she comes in and talks in broken Russian and moves around me seductively, when she calls me Gregorii. She says she is writing comedies on the side and that we need to be inoculated. I find myself calling her Luisa, leaning in for a kiss when there is none forthcoming. I taste mint when I wake in the morning.

Last night she brought several blades in a bucket into my room and had me put my forearm down on a towel. 'You're ill, my poor little king, here, let me bleed you and you can sleep it off.' The blades slid into my arm like a blessing.

♦

Tombstoned

home is where you hang
yourself, the line curled into the familiar
exotic, the house disseminated, no longer
integral, but exuding those same corrosive
emanations: the dank hallway decades away,
the cool basement of denial,
the pristine living room coping with cheap techniques,
the quiet acrid attic longing for deluge.

dwelling deep within this stranger
in a strange hand, the tornado prying
the shingles free, what is left
to do but suck in the cool corrugated roots,
the indivisible striations of rock?

walk in, my body rocking with treetops
toppling through my spine, there is
no return and a gift
passes for the moment,
disguised and anchored by grief.

even if you turn away,
your feet are wet and prints
tie the two events together.

♦

DARK RED FADE-IN, as if vibrantly coloured shutters have opened into a brightly lit space, to a video camera and tripod standing against a sheet-draped background. A DRY, RATTLING HUM suggests the camera is running. Perhaps the camera is facing a mirror; perhaps a second camera is doing the filming.

A VOICE-OVER by a male NARRATOR begins .

NARRATOR

Sometimes an artist just wants to say, I hope you will be safe, I hope you will be happy, I hope you will not be hurt, or, if you are hurt, wounded, lost, that you will find healing, you will find yourself, and, in the end, you will be at peace. So, I say this to you now. Be well, friend.

FADE TO BLACK.

♦

Reign

In the fall of 1771, I faced death in all its guises, all at once, and lived.

I said goodbye to my figchen in the Assumption Cathedral after saying prayers for the already dead in Moscow. She pleaded for me to stay, claimed she would order me not to go, but as Grand Master of the Ordnance, it was my duty. I knew I was not invincible – Ekaterina had taught me that – and, while I had had my 'heroic' moments, I did not consider myself a reckless hero. I felt compelled to pursue this crisis, felt that it, above anything else, threatened me and my figchen.

A plague was sweeping through Moscow – the scattered reports and fear could lead only to that conclusion. A leader had to travel to Moscow to organize containment and the orderly disposal of bodies before it spread across all of Russia. A hot, charged wind blew.

The world's body had gone mad with fever. I was to bleed it.

♦

I am not sure how this is going to translate; how do you translate writing into film? Or, for that matter, is 'translate' the right word? Either way, you are going to misinterpret this.

What I have been trying to say is that this is not unlike necrophilia. Dee and I lie naked on either side of Henry's body, stroking his white white mushroom skin, following the curvature of his flesh with our own. His body is stored in the cold room with the broccoli, covered with vegetable oil, honey wax, sprigs of basil and garlands of lilac blooms, wrapped in thick plastic taken from the greenhouse. We've taped up his eyes with bright shiny loonies over each and shaved off all his hair. We filled his mouth with cloves and nutmeg. Stitches still appear dark and garish against the skin of his belly, thighs and shoulders: these were the places where the library and then the bulldozer tore at him. His left hand is missing and there is a large bulging bandage covering that wrist.

The camera is running. It is a gentle homage – quiet, fluid, complex in its emotional energy. Lying there, with Dee and Henry, silently contemplative, I feel I have returned home for the first time in my life.

It is not surprising that Henry, finally, is among us, his presence not one.

It is here that I recollect my film. Lying here next to Henry, I reconstruct my passage (a careening truck, a camera mounted on it, precarious) here. Everything up until now has been past-tense, a warm-up to now, the present tense that I know fully. A death grip of knowledge.

♦

Dear Little King,

To tempt, and to be tempted, are things very nearly allied, and, in spite of the finest maxims of morality impressed upon the mind, whenever feeling has anything to do in the matter, no sooner is it excited than we have already gone vastly farther than we are aware of, and I have yet to learn how it is possible to prevent its being excited. Flight alone is, perhaps, the only remedy; but there are cases and circumstances in which flight becomes impossible, for how is it possible to fly, shun or turn one's back in the midst of a court? Now, if you do not fly, there is nothing, it seems to me, so difficult as to escape from that which is essentially agreeable. All that can be said in opposition to it will appear but a prudery quite out of harmony with the natural instincts of the human heart; besides, no one holds his heart in his hand, tightening or relaxing his grasp of it at pleasure. Gregorii, my dear, will you come to me without my summons? Are we nearing the end?

Yours, Fike

♦

The world seems to have receded now.

The world seems to have receded.

I (she, we, him – it hardly matters at this point) have drawn the blinds, unplugged the telephone. We seem to be cocooning. We seem to be cocooning ourselves in text, image, hermeneutics. Objects, simple objects on the kitchen table, a glass, a turnip, a ghostly hand, become signs, become representative of something else. This is not our house. This floor has become unstable.

I may have transformed myself in this time – it is hard to believe this; one always wonders if one would know. Might it, like many things, take two to make any metamorphosis possible. A tree falling in the forest. I walk past Dee's room and perpetually see her novel (now as tall as a person) standing there. She has disappeared or transformed as well. She may be the novel standing there. I occasionally open a shutter to see if the world is still there but only find myself looking at a film, at a theatre screen. The lights are all down in the house – the breakers snapped off at some point by Dee's hand. The cats have all left to find food. Plants are all overgrown, spreading madly across tables and windows. There seems to be an acceleration of things. I am shrinking and can't reach the top shelf of the cupboards where the mangoes ripen.

Sometimes, though, I am Gregorii and I have to stoop through doorways. Sometimes now I have breasts and a jewelled tiara. It is not surprising. It seems fitting.

Sometimes now I am older, dying, missing one finger. Sometimes now I am dead. It seems fitting.

When it is hot outside (this barely registered, the strange hot wind that has blown in from the southeast, a searing, scouring hot wind and the world is a technological question) Henry's skin becomes slightly rubbery, like a plum that has sat on the kitchen counter for a few days. He is surrounded by broccoli flowerets and bundles of carrots. The humidity enters his body like a sponge. Our sweat-streaked bodies sit astride him and we wonder about the precious power of mistake, the gorgeous pliancy of chance.

It seems as if the world may be ending, mushroom clouds hovering at the farthest reaches of the horizon.

It seems fitting.

And language starts. Sitting astride Henry, Dee and I, I and Dee, we and Henry, converse on the nature of language and death. Gazing upon his sunken chest, his knotted feet, his flaccid penis, his unforthcoming face, we are released from the thrall of empire, from the architectures of the rational. His body, that last vestige of manhood lying there pale and ungainly, becomes a conduit to a new language, a new being. That strange trickle of knowledge approaches from all around, space suddenly become stone, and the sign ascends. Test pattern.

♦

On the prow of the Tver at sunset she climbs up the railing and bids me to follow. We perch there, the water rushing under us, the wind bucking us sideways. Sometimes a life filters into the world's air so completely that details, settings like this one, fade away. I will never forget this time with my figchen, never. It is etched in my name, my name etched in history, history etched over and over. We stand there, teetering on the railing, two bodies on the edge of an interminable text.

She turns her head and says coolly, 'Let's go.'

♦

It was the last time we touched. History does not exist.

♦

A tender keeper this room, and I sit writing the last scene, the end of the script. Next to me, within easy reach, a tidy bottle of abstraction. Dee hovers at the door, ghostly in her own way, directing my hand. She is probably disappointed, frowning at my recalcitrant form, cursing under her breath. The camera is running, a constant wide-angle shot, the camera is always running now. Without words I ask her how to proceed, how to complete the film, how to end it. She leans on the doorframe, regards me for small spans of time, comes and goes beyond me. My quest (such a droll word – history carrying it away) leads to my quiet oblivion, that other place where I enter the film fully, where I can meet Dee in abandonment. Pace, breath, closure. The question becomes, am I part of the script, am I in it?

The question becomes, where will I go?

A noise by the door … Dee?

'Oh, hello Henry.'

♦

> coursing, preemptive breath taking
> hold of the imprint, that slight impression
> on paper, rhythms of conduct, the last
> catheter taking one outside one
> self-determined to drift, an epoch inclination
> a continent unearthed as revision
> tremors in the steep land-locked
> languages of sense, futurity, the wrinkles
> left by pictures bright but unremembered
>
> cut, there is no apocalypse that dreams
> that fear, that closeness, that fallopian
> gasp of recognition – it is clutched, an enigma

mid-rift, an organ swamped with nerves and
that ecstatic panic of text; it is that which saves time,
turns one's gaze into stone, sun
warmed, unassuming, fleetingly alive
astride the scene, the set,

(camera still) the ultimate asceticism —
so completely that the body erupts into the past
dissevers, an ancient, poised aposiopesis
enabling another

FADE TO BLACK.

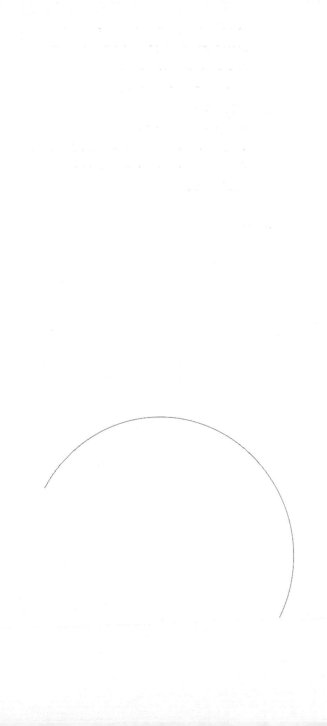

Acknowledgements

I would like to thank Debbie Keahey, the UNBC Office of Research and the Manitoba Arts Council for support during the writing and publishing of this novel.

Thanks to Alana Wilcox for her intuitive and tireless editing. She made me realize that the novel was *about* tenses — in what tense do you speak of a dead person? And thanks to Jason McBride and the rest of Coach House Books. CH is the best press in Canada.

Thanks to Robert Kroetsch and Aritha van Herk for providing such amazing texts to respond to.

Thanks to my friend Andrew Riechel for an early reading that gave me faith in ambiguity and confidence in my inability to end the story.

Thanks to Gwen MacDonald for her support of my work and Lana Diaz for her help with the Spanish phrases, gracias.

Research into the life of Catherine the Great was aided by:

Alexander, John T. *Catherine the Great: Life and Legend*. New York: Oxford University Press, 1989.

Anthony, Katharine. *Catherine the Great*. Garden City, NY: Garden City Publishing Company, 1925.

Kaus, Gina. *Catherine: The Portrait of an Empress*. New York:
    The Viking Press, 1935.
In the novel, I alter facts and dates frequently, and I, like Dee,
thought these biographies were crap.

Research into magic mushrooms and their religious implica-
tions included references to:
Wasson, R. Gordon, George Cowan, Florence Cowan and
    Willard Rhodes. *Maria Sabina and Her Mazatec Mushroom
    Velada*.
    New York: Harcourt Brace Jovanovich, 1974.
Wasson, R. Gordon. *The Wondrous Mushroom: Mycolatry in
    Mesoamerica*. New York: McGraw-Hill, 1980.

The poem on page 75 appears in a slightly different form in
Budde, Robert. *Catch as Catch*. Winnipeg: Turnstone, 1995.

Page 99 quotes Neruda, Pablo. *Passions and Impressions*. Trans.
Magaret Sayers Peden. New York: Farrar Straus Giroux, 1978.

An excerpt of *The Dying Poem* appeared in *The Cyclops Review*
(2002), edited by Jon Paul Fiorentino and Clive Holden from
Cyclops Press in Winnipeg.

Rob Budde teaches creative writing at the University of Northern British Columbia in Prince George. He has published three books: poetry collections *Catch as Catch* and *traffick* and the novel *Misshapen*. He has been a finalist for the John Hirsch Award for Most Promising Manitoba Writer and the McNally-Robinson Manitoba Book of the Year. In 1995, Budde completed a Ph.D. in Creative Writing at the University of Calgary. Check out his online literary journal called stonestone <http://stonestone.unbc.ca>.

Typeset in Spectrum
Printed and bound at the Coach House on bpNichol Lane, 2002

Edited and designed by Alana Wilcox
Cover design by Bill Kennedy
Cover photo by Danny Ouellette

To read the online version of the text, visit our website:
www.chbooks.com

Send us a request to be added to our email list:
mail@chbooks.com

Call us toll-free:
1 800 367 6360

Coach House Books
401 Huron Street (rear) on bpNichol Lane
Toronto ON
M5S 2G5